DOOM
TRAIL

Center Point
Large Print

Also by Bradford Scott and available from
Center Point Large Print:

Ranger Daring
Border War
Outlaw Land
Powder Burn
Texas Rider
Guns of the Alamo
The Slick-Iron Trail
Lone Star Rider

**This Large Print Book carries the
Seal of Approval of N.A.V.H.**

DOOM TRAIL

A Walt Slade Western

Bradford Scott

CENTER POINT LARGE PRINT
THORNDIKE, MAINE

1

"Walter J. Slade, stand up and hear your sentence!"

Ranger Walt Slade, whom the Mexican *peones* of the Rio Grande river villages named *El Halcón*—The Hawk—rose to his feet and faced the judge's glower firmly.

"Slade," said the judge, "you have been convicted of two deliberate killings, by a jury of your peers; is there any reason why sentence should not be passed on you?"

"Guess not," Slade admitted.

"Very well. I hereby sentence you to imprisonment for a period of one hour in the Hogwaller saloon. And furthermore, that you buy the court and the jury a drink!"

The courtroom rocked with laughter. "Sheriff!" roared the judge, "take those two carcasses out an plant 'em! Court's adjourned!"

He stood up, grinning at Slade. "Come on, Walt, let's go get that drink," he said. "Told you we'd find you guilty and that you'd get a stiff sentence."

"No more than I deserve, I guess," Slade conceded. "I missed one shot."

They left the courtroom together, admiring glances following El Halcón's tall form. Coroner

Tom Bowles—courtesy title "judge"—chuckled as they crossed the street. But before they reached the saloon in question he was grave.

"A joke's a joke, Walt, and we have to have a little fun now and then, but just the same it's a darn serious matter," he said. "Sure as blazes you downed two of Tarp Henry's killers, and Henry will be out to even the score."

"Wouldn't be surprised," conceded Slade, who did not appear overly impressed.

"Blast it!" snorted Bowles, "haven't you got a nerve in your body? You're up against what would send most men skalleyhooting out of the section, and you treat *it* as if it were a joke. Tarp Henry is the most dangerous, the most vicious, and the smartest outlaw this section has ever known, and it's known plenty."

"Well, if that pair he sent to do a killing last night were the best he had, I figure there's not too much to worry about," Slade returned composedly.

"The next time he's liable to send a half dozen," Bowles said pointedly. "Why in blazes don't you reveal that you're a Ranger instead of mavericking around wearing that loco El Halcón owl-hoot brand? Even Henry would hesitate to murder a Texas Ranger."

"That's just the point, Tom," Slade replied. "If he knows a Ranger is on his trail, he'll cover up, maybe pull out, which I don't want to happen—

it would mean another long and arduous chase. While if he believes I'm just another owlhoot trying to horn in on his preserves, I figure he'll get careless and perhaps tip his hand."

"And, meanwhile, you may well lean against the hot tip of a slug," Bowles said meaningfully. "Well, I guess there's no use giving you good advice; you won't take it, and somehow you always manage to dodge the loop. Some particular devil must look after his own. Here we are, and I need that drink. You make me jumpy."

They entered the saloon, the six members of the coroner's jury filing in behind them. Angelo Murphy, who had been present at the inquest, hurried forward to greet them. Murphy, better known as Wingless Angel, was the proprietor of the Hogwaller.

"I'll pay the prisoner's fine," he announced. "Pete, fill 'em up, on the house."

"Fine suspended," chuckled Bowles. "Here's to more and better inquests, gents."

Slade sipped his drink and chatted with the jurymen; but Bowles was still bothered and kept casting glances at the swinging doors. Slade read his thoughts.

"Don't worry, Tom," he said. "They won't make another try so soon. Besides, if there is another one, I figure it will be something more subtle, not a direct approach to shoot it out."

"Loco terrapin brains!" snorted Bowles.

"Thinking they could shade the fastest gunhand in the whole Southwest!"

"They didn't do too bad," Slade replied. "And odds of two to one are always a mite lopsided; you can only take care of one at a time."

"That's right," agreed Bowles. "How's your arm?"

"Nothing to it," Slade answered. "Doc McChesney took a couple of stitches and put on a strip of plaster; it'll be okay in a day or two."

"Hope so," said Bowles. "You're likely to need it. Well, now we'll have a drink on His Honor the Court. Fill 'em up again, Pete."

"And then I'm going to have a cup of coffee and something to eat," Slade announced.

"Me, too," said Bowles. "Inquests are always hungry affairs. I see a vacant table over there."

Wingless Angel escorted them to the table in question.

"Hope you won't figure this one an unlucky table, Mr. Slade," he said.

"On the contrary, I consider it a very lucky table," Slade replied smilingly. "It served its purpose well last night."

Wingless chuckled and beckoned a waiter.

"Hot coffee first, then everything you've got, we're famished," Slade told the waiter. "Court proceedings sharpen the appetite."

Bowles thrust a tentative fingertip in a splintered hole in the table top.

"This was it, eh?" he remarked.

"Yes, that was the one that came all the way through and nicked my arm," Slade answered. "It was pretty well spent after passing through the thick oak top, though. Which was fortunate for me. Otherwise, it might have hit me a lot harder lick."

Bowles nodded. "Wouldn't be surprised," he agreed. "Walt, just what did happen and what led up to it? All those horned toads who testified at the inquest seemed to have a different version to tell. The only things they agreed on was that you shot in self-defense and that they were sure those two hellions belonged to Tarp Henry's bunch. Suppose you give me the straight of it."

"Okay," Slade said, sipping the coffee the waiter brought. Here goes . . .

The sun was setting like unheard thunder of scarlet and gold behind the topmost crags of the Cap Rock, as Walt Slade rode into Signal. Surrounded by the hills of the Cap Rock, Signal drowsed peacefully in the dying light, like an old hombre wrapped in a colorful serape who nevertheless had a knife under the blanket and a gun within reach. Signal's *peace* was deceptive.

Directly ahead, the twin steel ribbons of the railroad shimmered darkly red. Slade pulled Shadow, his tall black horse, to a halt as a big locomotive boomed out of the east with crackling exhaust and clanging siderods, pulling a long train of rocking freight cars. The air filled with the pungent whiff of sulphur and hot oil, and the fragrance of new grain and fresh fruit. Slade waited until the caboose bobbed past, its rear markers glowing and winking westward. Then he rode on along Signal's crooked main street, which was a portion of the old Butterick east-west trail.

On his way to Signal, Slade had paused at several towns, including Stanfield, less than twenty miles to the west. In each of them the tall, broad-shouldered, deep-chested man with the lean, deeply bronzed hawk face dominated by cold eyes of a pale gray fringed with long black lashes had attracted more than a little attention. At some, including Stanfield, he had been recognized.

"That's El Halcón, the outlaw that's always too smart to get caught," ran the low mutter. "Fastest gunhand in the whole Southwest, or so they say. Singingest man in the whole Southwest, too. That's what everybody who's heard him says."

"Fine-looking feller, ain't he?"

"Uh-huh, he sure is, but hope he don't decide to stop here. Trouble just follows that big jigger around."

"Got killings to his credit, ain't he?"

"So they say. Funny, though, about everybody he's killed sure had a killing coming, or so they say."

"Not so loud; he mightn't like being gabbed about."

"Sure wouldn't want to get him riled. Look the way those two guns are slung."

"Uh-huh, and notice his hands don't ever seem to be far away from them. A funny jigger, all right, and hard to figure. Lots of folks swear by him, some of them mighty nice folks, and all the Mexicans do."

"Mexicans may be ornery, some of 'em, but they're mighty good at sizin' a feller up right. Those eyes of his go through you like a greased knife. But if he happens to smile, his whole face changes, eyes, too, and you get a feeling you just got to smile back. Yep, a funny jigger."

And so it went.

2

Slade's first thought was a stable for his horse, which he located without difficulty. After properly introducing the stablekeeper— for without Slade's okay, nobody could lay a hand on the big black—and making sure all Shadow's needs were properly provided for, Slade sallied forth in search of something to eat. A wide window with HOGWALLER legended across it in red caught his eye and caused him to chuckle. Over the swinging doors came a cheerful sound of bottle necks clinking on glass rims, intermingled with strains of music played by a better than average orchestra, and a cheerful gabble of conversation. Also, of more interest to a hungry man, the aroma of boiling coffee and frying meat. He decided that the Hogwaller, despite its rather questionable name, must be okay. Without hesitation he entered, to find himself in a large and brightly lighted room that boasted a long bar, well crowded, a dance floor, poker tables, a couple of roulette wheels and a faro bank. There were also a lunch counter and tables for more leisurely diners.

Slade spotted a vacant table from which he would have a clear view of the door and sat down there. A waiter, smiling and nodding, took his order. Soon an appetizing meal was placed before him. He ate slowly and with relish, ordered a final cup of coffee and rolled a cigarette with the slender fingers of his left hand. Then, well fed and content, he leaned back comfortably in his chair and studied the busy room.

Most of the occupants were cowhands, largely fresh-faced young fellows, gay and reckless but with no real harm in them. There was also quite a sprinkling of railroaders, Signal being a division point. Slade knew that when the railroad was building through, some years before, Signal had seen some high old times. Cowboys had shot up the town regularly and were in continual combat with the railroad construction workers until the line moved operations west. In those days saloons way outnumbered other business establishments. Things had changed somewhat and now the ratio was about fifty-fifty. Signal had cooled down a bit, but not too much. The Cap Rock region always had been and doubtless always would be sanctuary for outlaws and other gentlemen who preferred to do their riding between the hours of sunset and dawn . . . of whom it appeared there were a few in Hogwaller at the moment.

They, however, were pretty good at minding their own business and not bothering anybody who did not interfere with them.

Slade was still smoking and sipping his coffee

when the two men entered, pushing through the swinging doors and fanning out on either side of them. They were lean, hard-faced men with watchful eyes, and the way their guns were slung said plainly to the initiated that they were not worn as ornaments. Slade leaned forward a trifle, his hands hooked under the table top.

The pair swept the room with their glance, undoubtedly in search of somebody; their gaze focused on Slade's table. For an instant they stared. Then their hands flashed down and the formerly orderly establishment exploded in a whirlwind action.

Over went the table, Slade behind it, both guns blazing over the edge. Answering bullets hammered the thick oaken boards of the top. One of the gunmen screamed, a horrible gurgling shriek, and pitched forward on his face, blood gushing from his bullet-slashed throat. A slug pierced the table top and Slade reeled slightly from the shock as the lead nicked his left arm.

The second killer turned as if to run, then sank to the floor in a huddled heap and did not move.

Slade was on his feet, a smoking gun in each hand. His icy gaze swept the gathering. Under that bleak glare, men who a moment before were struggling wildly to get out of line, stood rigid, hands motionless.

"Take it easy, cowboy," a voice shouted. "Us fellers ain't in on this."

With another glance around, Slade holstered his guns, righted the overturned table, drew up a chair and sat down.

"I think I can use a little more coffee," he said to a white-faced and apparently paralyzed waiter who stood as if rooted to the floor.

"Some more coffee, please," Slade repeated, in a slightly louder voice.

The waiter jumped as if just discovering he was sitting on an aroused tarantula.

"Yes-yes, s-sir! Coming right—right up, sir!" He headed for the kitchen at a run. Slade's lips twitched and with a handkerchief he swabbed at the blood trickling over his left hand, felt tentatively of his upper arm, where a bullet tear showed in his shirt sleeve, and shrugged.

The Hogwaller proprietor, making his way through the crowd to the table, glanced at Slade's bloody hand, turned and beckoned a swamper, who a moment later hurried through the swinging doors. The proprietor, big, good-humored-looking, but with alert eyes, paused and nodded to Slade.

"Good work, feller," he said. "I saw it all; those two skunks came in looking for it. Glad they found it, in a way they didn't expect. But, feller," he added, lowering his voice, "I'm scairt you've started something bad. Folks at the bar are saying that's a pair of Tarp Henry's killers."

"And who is Tarp Henry?" Slade asked, although he already knew.

"He's a blasted outlaw who's been raising hell and shoving a chunk under a corner hereabouts of late," growled Wingless Angel, the proprietor.

"That so?" Slade commented, sipping the coffee that the still shaking waiter brought.

Wingless stared, but before he could say more, a voice shouted, "Here comes the sheriff!"

Sheriff Dolf Chester was big and bulky and middle-aged, and looked worried. He gazed down at the two dead men for a moment, then lumbered over to Slade's table.

"Why did those jiggers want to kill you?" he asked abruptly.

"Your guess is as good as mine," Slade replied. "Perhaps they didn't like the way I comb my hair."

The sheriff flushed. "Don't get funny," he rumbled, "this is a serious matter."

"*Was* a serious matter," Slade corrected. "It isn't any more."

A chuckle ran through the crowd. Somebody sniggered out loud. Sheriff Chester flushed a darker red, but before he could word an angry retort, he was shoved aside by a lean, white-whiskered, red-faced old fellow who carried a small satchel.

"Hello, Doc, here he is," said Wingless.

Doc McChesney leaned forward, peered closer.

16

"Well, I might have known it!" he said. "How are you, Walt?" He thrust out a gnarled old hand and they shook.

"You know him?" broke in the sheriff.

"Sure I know him, what of it?" snorted the doctor. "Get out of my way."

The sheriff looked baffled, and moved aside.

"All right, off with the shirt and let's have a look," said Doc. "Never mind that 'just a scratch' stuff. Do as I say."

Biting back a grin, Slade obeyed, baring his sinewy shoulders and corded arms. There was a gash across the left biceps. The crowd pressed closer to see.

Doc McChesney snapped open his satchel and drew forth what appeared to be a charged hypodermic needle.

"This thing's loaded with smallpox germs," he observed sententiously. "The first hellion that gets in my way is going to get a jab with it. Give me room!"

He got room.

A cleansing, a couple of stitches and a strip of plaster, and Doc said, "Okay, that'll hold you."

Slade donned his shirt and ordered more coffee. Doc consented to have a cup with him.

Meanwhile, Wingless Angel and Sheriff Chester were deep in conversation. The sheriff nodded and returned to the table.

" 'Pears you were justified, but stick around for

the inquest tomorrow, the coroner will want to hold one," he said to Slade.

"He'll be there," said Doc McChesney. "He's going over to my place for the night."

"All right," said the sheriff. With a last look at Slade, his brows drawing together as if in perplexity, he walked off to arrange for having the bodies packed out.

"How come you're here, Doc?" Slade asked. "Thought I left you in Abilene."

"You did," the doctor replied, "but folks were getting too darn healthy over there, and nobody was getting shot. So I came over here where things are different. Remember Tom Bowles? Thought you would. He came along with me. Got himself elected coroner last year. He'll be tickled pink to see you, but betcha he pulls something. That hellion will manage somehow to make a joke of his own funeral."

Slade laughed. Tom Bowles was notorious as a practical joker.

"Doc," he said suddenly, "what do you know about Tarp Henry?"

"Well," replied McChesney, "he's getting to be something of a legend hereabouts. He robs prospectors, sometimes kills them. Held up the stage from Lubbock a couple of times. Wrecked a train and robbed the express car. Killed the express messenger. Or at least everybody figures it was Henry and his bunch."

"Let an outlaw bunch start getting a reputation and they are blamed for everything off-color that happens," Slade commented.

Doc nodded. "That's right," he agreed, "but in Henry's case I've a notion he doesn't get blamed for much for which he isn't responsible. He's bad, and he's smart. Lots of cows been missing of late. They say Henry wide-loops them and runs them across to New Mexico and the mountains. Who is he, where does he come from? Nobody seems to know for sure. Some folks swear he's old Jesse James come back to life. The James brothers, Frank and Jesse, had a horse ranch down to the southeast of here and used it as a hideout."

"I rather doubt that Jesse has come back to life," Slade smiled.

"Doesn't seem reasonable," conceded Doc, "but from all I been able to gather, Tarp Henry is worse than Jesse ever was. McNelty send you down here after Henry?"

"A lot of reports and complaints have been coming in to the Post," Slade replied. "Captain Jim thought it might be a good notion for me to take a look."

"McNelty has sense," grunted Doc. "But don't underestimate Henry. What happened tonight is a sample of how he works. If he figures somebody is in his way, he eliminates them. I suppose he found out you are El Halcón and decided you came here to horn in on his good thing."

"Wouldn't be surprised," Slade conceded.

"Chester will hear you are El Halcón and, the chances are, will be snortin' around tomorrow," continued Doc. "Don't pay him no mind; dumb but honest. A tough cow country sheriff, but he was sorta behind the door when they were handing out brains. Against such a specimen as Tarp Henry he's hopeless. Got sense enough to realize it, though; that's why he wrote to McNelty asking for help . . . which is to his credit. Well, ready for bed?"

"I'll fetch my pouches from the stable and be with you," Slade agreed. "I figured the owner dependable."

"He is," said McChesney. "Okay, let's go."

They left the saloon together, all eyes following, Wingless Angel tugging hard on his handle-bar mustache.

3

"And that," Slade said to his attentive listener, "is just about the whole story, Tom."

"I see," nodded Bowles. "Well, Doc and I both put bugs in Chester's ear when he started complaining that he had enough trouble without El Halcón squattin' in his bailiwick. I reckon he figured you and Henry would end up doing for each other, which would be all to the good, from his point of view. Imagine you'll give him the lowdown on what you really are when the time comes."

"Yes, when and if the times comes," Slade agreed. "Waiter, some more coffee."

They ate their meal mostly in silence, as is usually the way with hungry men who have known what it is to find good food scarce. Later, over cigarettes, the talk came back to Tarp Henry.

"Tom, what do you really know about Henry?" Slade asked.

"Well," replied Bowles, "about as much and as little as anybody, I suppose. Seems he started out robbing and murdering prospectors for their gold. Plenty of gold in the hills for those who know where to look for it. Good placer mining country, and metal can be panned from the creek beds. Henry sort of specialized in prospectors for a while. Those who wouldn't tell where their gold was hidden he pegged naked over ant hills or crucified them to the spines of cholla cactus until they were ready to talk. Usually he murdered them after he learned what he wanted to know. Then he started branching out, stage and train robberies, and a bank. Cattle have been wide-looped and everybody says Henry is responsible. The devil only knows where he'll bust loose next."

"What about his personal appearance?" Slade asked.

"A few prospectors who got away from him alive, and passengers on that train he wrecked and robbed, say a big, tall, broad-shouldered hellion with black hair and eyes 'peared to be giving the orders," Bowles replied. "Guess that was Henry, all right."

"Not much to go on," Slade commented. "Well, we'll see. Looks like he employs the time-honored outlaw method of ruling by terror. Gets folks afraid to talk."

"That's so," agreed Bowles. "Mention his name and a lot of folks will tighten the *látigos* on their jaws, pronto. Some of 'em are looking sorta sideways at you right now, because you downed that pair last night folks figure belonged to the Henry bunch. Reckon they'd rather not be seen in your company."

Slade laughed. Bowles added a chuckle.

At that moment a slender, elegant-looking man of medium height entered the saloon. He wore the conservative garb of a prosperous rancher and was extremely good-looking with yellow hair, deep-blue eyes and straight features. He glanced about, spotted Bowles and waved a cordial greeting before making his way to the bar.

"Now there's a really nice feller," said Bowles. "That's Allen Curtis who bought the Forked S spread from old Branch Stanton about eight or nine months back. We've been getting quite a few newcomers hereabouts of late. Several of them are titled Englishmen, like those up in Montana. Remittance men they're called. Get money sent them from home as long as they'll just stay away, I gather. Sorta black sheep of respectable families, as the saying goes."

Slade nodded his understanding; he had met the type.

"Curtis a remittance man?" he asked.

"Don't think so, though he might be," Bowles replied. "I doubt it, though, he knows the cow business too well. Don't know for sure just where he's from—never heard him say. He's okay, though, a plumb nice jigger. Gets along with everybody and always ready to lend a helping hand. A fine hombre."

Abruptly he ceased speaking and leaned forward in his chair.

"And talk about contrasts!" he exclaimed.

"Here comes a hellion who's just everything Curtis ain't. They're next-door neighbors, too, but they don't get along over well. That's Val Parker who owns the Bar Cross. He's another newcomer—showed up last year. Worked all over, to hear him tell it. Managed to get together enough *dinero* to buy a small spread from one of those English fellers I was telling you about who decided to pull out. Hot-tempered, quarrelsome. Been in several ruckuses. Sheriff finally threatened to bar him from town if he didn't behave. Sorta cooled down of late, but he'll bust loose again sooner or later, you can bet on that."

Val Parker looked in line with what Bowles described. He was big, thick-shouldered, long-armed, on the hulking side. He wore cowhand garb much the same as Slade's, though less neat—Levi's, scuffed half-boots of soft, tanned leather, faded blue shirt, vivid handkerchief looped about his corded neck. A battered, broad-brimmed "J.B." was tipped truculently over one flashing dark eye. He had a big-nosed face with high cheek bones, a wide, thick-lipped mouth. He walked with a definite swagger to the bar, pounded on it and demanded a drink. The bartender who poured it regarded him with evident disfavor.

"We get all sorts," sighed Bowles. "Well, now what?"

"I think I'll go out and walk around for a bit,"

Slade decided. "Still a couple of hours till dark. And you?"

"Oh, I'll be getting back to my shop," Bowles answered. "I run a feed store when I haven't anything else to do. Want to take a look? Right down the street a few doors."

Slade was agreeable to the invitation and they left the saloon together. Watching the reflections in the back bar mirror, Slade saw Val Parker turn and follow them with his eyes.

Bowles's feed store was small but well stocked, and he employed two clerks. Slade knew him to be an excellent businessman with a penchant for dabbling in politics. He met the clerks, looked things over, and promised Bowles he'd meet him in the Hogwaller after he closed up shop. Then he sauntered out and wandered about the town, which he found interesting.

Signal was still a typical Texas cowtown. Long hitchracks lined the dusty streets, with cayuses drowsing beside them while their riders sought food, or something else. About every other building housed a saloon. Most of the buildings had false fronts and many of them were already weather-beaten. Later, oil refineries, cotton gins and natural gas distribution would boom the *pueblo*, but at present, cattle was the mainstay of business.

There were plenty of people on the street— cowhands in the careless but efficient garb of the rangeland, well-dressed ranch owners and business people, gamblers and dealers in sober black relieved by the snow of ruffled shirt fronts, dance-floor girls who eyed him with decided favor, prospectors in patched overalls, floppy and battered hats on their heads, dreams in their eyes. These last Slade regarded with smiling understanding. They were the true Magi and endowed with the true wisdom, he thought. Content with the present. Looking forward to the future, the big strike, the fabulous lode—dreams seldom realized, but the prospectors were happy in their dreaming. What more could one desire!

People turned to gaze at the tall man with the steady gray eyes, the thick, crisp black hair and the rather wide mouth—grin-quirked at the corners—that somewhat relieved the tinge of fierceness evinced by the prominent hawk nose above and the lean, powerful jaw and chin beneath, struck by the rhythmic perfection of his movement. Many recognized him as El Halcón, he knew, and were discussing in low tones his exploit of the night before.

Which was what he desired. He didn't know where to look for Tarp Henry and his bunch, but he figured that perhaps his El Halcón reputation might bring Tarp Henry to him. Which would simplify matters.

Due to his working under cover as much as

possible and often not revealing his Ranger connections, Walt Slade had built up a peculiar dual reputation. "The smartest and most fearless Ranger of them all," said those who knew the truth. Others, who did not, were wont to declare profanely that El Halcón was just an owlhoot with too much savvy to get caught, so far.

Which, as Captain McNelty, the famed Commander of the Border Battalion, pointed out, laid him open to grave personal danger. Slade in turn would point out that it also opened up avenues of valuable information which would be closed to a known Ranger. So Captain Jim would grumble, Slade would laugh, and go his carefree way as El Halcón, "the friend of the lowly and the oppressed!"

The sun, a golden-maned stallion seeking rest, paced slowly down the pastures of the sky. The western crags closed behind him like corral bars dropping into place. The lovely blue dusk sifted down from the hilltops like impalpable dust. The lights of Signal winked cheery greeting to the blossoming stars. The stream of life quickened under the cool hands of night. The marts of business closed. The "palaces" of pleasure opened wide their arms. Signal's daytime hum crescendoed to the invitation of the dark.

When Slade entered the Hogwaller, some time later, Tom Bowles was already comfortably seated at a table, a glass in front of him.

Occupying another chair was Allen Curtis, the Forked S owner.

Bowles beckoned and Slade walked over to the table. Bowles performed the introductions and Slade and Curtis shook hands. Slade sensed that the rancher's slender, rather delicate-looking hand was strong as woven steel.

"Take a load off your feet, Walt," Bowles said, pulling out a chair. "We were just talking about the cow business hereabouts."

Slade sat down and for a while they discussed range matters, Curtis speaking in a pleasantly modulated voice. After some little time had passed, he glanced at the clock over the bar.

"Have to be getting back to my holding," he said, rising to his feet. "Busy day ahead of me tomorrow. Good night, Tom. Good night, Mr. Slade. It is a pleasure to know you." With a nod and a smile he left the saloon.

"A nice feller, all right," remarked Bowles.

"Appears to be," Slade agreed, glancing toward the bar, where he had already noted Val Parker, who owned the Bar Cross ranch and of whom Bowles did not approve. He had also noticed that Parker frequently turned to gaze in their direction. He was slightly surprised, however, when Parker left the bar and approached the table.

"Name's Slade, isn't it?" he asked without preamble, his voice deep and rumbling but not unmusical. "Mine's Parker—Val Parker. Heard about what you did in here last night. A good chore. It's gratifying to know that somebody has the courage to give front to those hellions. Too many people hereabouts shake in their shoes when Tarp Henry's name is mentioned."

"Thank you, Mr. Parker," Slade replied. Parker nodded.

"Planning to remain in the section a while?" he asked.

"I haven't made up my mind yet just how long I'll remain," Slade answered.

"If you are and are looking for a chore of riding, you can find one with me," Parker said. "I can use a top hand or two, but they're not easy to come by in this section."

"Thank you, Mr. Parker," Slade repeated. "I'll think on it, if I decide to remain any length of time."

"Offer stands," said Parker. "Hope you'll see fit to regard it favorably." With a nod he returned to the bar.

"Well, what do you think of him?" Bowles asked curiously.

"I don't know," Slade admitted frankly. "His choice of words and his manner of expressing himself are not exactly what one would expect from a man who supposedly has spent all his life as a cowhand."

"A queer duck, all right," Bowles observed. "Knows the cow business, no doubt about that.

But as you say, somehow he's different from the average rider, although he gives the impression that ranch work is all he's ever done. Well, what's next?"

"Next I'm going to have something to eat, and then I think I'll head for Doc's place and go to bed," Slade replied. "I plan a little ride into the hills tomorrow, and I want to get an early start."

"Better keep your eyes skinned," Bowles advised. "Tarp Henry is supposed to have a hang-out somewhere in those hills."

"I'll try," Slade promised and beckoned a waiter.

4

Slade's notion of early was a trifle drastic, to put it mildly. Two hours before dawn he made his way to the stable through the deserted streets and put the rig on Shadow. The town was silent with sleep, with only here and there a glimmer of light. After a glance around, he rode west at a steady pace. On the crest of a rise a mile distant he pulled up and gazed long and earnestly back the way he had come.

"Don't appear to be wearing a tail," he told the horse.

Shadow snorted agreement and ambled on.

Slade was well into the hills when the sun rose. He slowed the big black and studied the terrain over which he passed. Everywhere were silence and desolation, the stillness broken only by the morning chirp of birds and the soft soughing of the wind in the trees.

Since the beginning of time this had been a wild land. The Indians and those before them had crisscrossed it with trails, most of them now but faint tracks. Here prospectors roamed and hunted men found sanctuary. The abrupt escarpment of the Cap Rock, with a zone of broken country below, called the breaks, extended west to the New Mexico Line and southward from the northernmost limit of the Panhandle to the Pecos Valley, with altitudes of from three thousand to near five thousand feet. Here, where Slade rode, it was extremely rugged, and largely brush covered.

Several hours after sunrise, still riding at a leisurely pace, he reached a point where the trail he was following forked. One branch curved into a dense stand of chaparral only a few hundred yards distant. And suddenly came a stutter of shots not far off and swiftly drawing nearer.

"Now what in blazes!" he exclaimed, pulling Shadow to a halt.

While he was still undecided what to do or what could be the meaning of the uproar, two mules came tearing from the growth.

A big *aparejo* or rawhide pack saddle, bounced and jolted on the back of one. On the back of the other bounced and jolted a man whose gray whiskers flared out on either side. He wore patched and faded garments. There were holes in his battered hat and his laced boots were scuffed and run over at heel. The run-over heels beat a frantic tattoo on the ribs of the speeding mule.

"What in blazes!" Slade repeated in astonishment. Instinctively his hand dropped to the butt of the heavy Winchester snugged in the saddle boot beneath his left thigh. He stared at the approaching rider. Then his attention was distracted elsewhere.

Out of the brush bulged five more riders mounted on racing horses. From their close-packed ranks spurted puffs of smoke. The boom of the guns flung back from the hillside.

Even as Slade stared, and tightened his grip on the rifle, the end came. The lead mule gave an almost human scream and went down in a twitching heap. The rider was flung over its head to lie writhing and struggling on the trail. From the pursuers came exultant whoops which were abruptly knifed through by a yell of warning as the gun slingers sighted Slade sitting his black horse at the edge of the trail. And the next instant Slade found himself in the middle of the ruckus. The horsemen jerked their mounts to a halt. Smoke puffed again. Lead yelled through the air.

But it yelled through the space Slade had occupied the second before. He had seen the gleam of shifted metal and left the saddle in a streak of movement, sliding the Winchester free as he went down.

"Git, Shadow!" he snapped as he hit the ground. The black instantly leaped sideways into the brush. Slade flopped behind a convenient shallow ridge.

Walt Slade didn't like being shot at by total strangers and signified his displeasure in no uncertain terms. Fire streamed from the muzzle of the Winchester.

The foremost horseman wore a big silver buckle in the center of his middle. The buckle stood out hard and clear against the front sight of Slade's rifle. The Winchester bucked and its wearer left the saddle as if swept from it by a mighty hand. Slade shifted the rifle muzzle the merest trifle. Bullets were kicking up the dust all around him, but he refused to be flustered. The plunging of a frightened horse spoiled his aim a trifle, but as the rifle cracked he saw the leg of a second rider jerk wildly to the accompaniment of a howl of pain. Slade fired again, saw a third man sway.

The gray-whiskered rider of the dead mule had managed to make it to his hands and knees and scuttled into a clump of brush like a scared rabbit. And from the clump came a tremendous boom and a cloud of smoke. Slade saw the face of the foremost horseman whipped to a bloody smear as a slug tore his upper lip and the lower part of his nose to shreds of flesh. He bubble-screamed blood and curses, whirled his horse and fled madly back the way he had come, his three companions streaming behind him, the leg of one flapping loosely. Slade sped them on their way with a couple more shots that sent a hat sailing through the air. From the brush clump came a second volcanic explosion and another cloud of smoke as the discomfited quartette disappeared into the chaparral.

Slade stood up, his rifle ready for action. From the brush clump peered a black muzzle about the size of a small nail keg. It was followed by a bewhiskered face. The mule rider stepped into view, in his hand an enormous horse pistol.

"Uncock that cannon, old-timer," Slade said. "You're liable to blow the hill over."

The other man chuckled creakily and let the hammer down. He was a little old man who jerked forward with a pronounced limp.

"Much obliged, cowboy," he called in his creaky voice. "Reckon you saved my bacon for me."

"Perhaps," Slade conceded, sliding fresh cartridges into the magazine of the Winchester. "However, it was a sort of personal affair; the hellions threw lead at me, too."

"So I noticed," the old-timer admitted, with another rusty chuckle. "Reckon they throw lead at anybody who gets in their way."

"Well, they collected a little this time," Slade observed, adding casually, "any ideas who they were?"

"Some of Tarp Henry's owlhoots," the oldster replied without hesitation. "Don't think Tarp was with 'em. Just one of his raiding parties on the lookout for prospectors headin' for town. Sort of keeping an eye on me, maybe."

"Looked like they were trying to do more than keep an eye on you," Slade observed. "Mighty

35

lucky for you the slug that did for the mule wasn't a bit higher."

The old fellow hesitated, looked him up and down with his faded but shrewd eyes.

"It was the mules they were after," he said.

"The mules?"

"Uh-huh," replied the other, holstering his horse pistol and worrying off a chaw from a black slab of eatin' tobacco. "There's a sorta plump poke snugged down in that pack saddle. I was heading for town to put it in the bank and fill up the pack with chuck and stuff I need."

"I see," Slade nodded. "Some of Tarp Henry's men, I believe you said. Who's Tarp Henry?"

The old man's eyes flashed. "The meanest outlaw that ever hit this section," he replied. "Leaning against the hot end of a bullet is the easy way if Tarp Henry is after you. He has some mighty unpleasant ways of doing in folks, especially if he can't get 'em to tell him what he wants to know."

Slade nodded again, and decided to let that angle pass for the time being. He figured the old-timer was not one to rush but would come through with information if given time. He knew he was being sized up and felt sure he'd pass inspection. Then the prospector would very likely open up. He *might* know something of value. He was speaking again.

"Reckon I'll head back to my shack in a

draw—just a couple of miles—and pick up another mule 'fore making another try for town," he said. "You come along with me if you hanker for a surroundin' of good chuck. Reckon you do. Cowhands are always hungry, that's been my experience with 'em. I'd like to get the hull off the dead mule first, though. Son, my name's Grady, Ben Grady. Mostly known as Uncle Ben. I like to be called Uncle Ben."

"Okay, Uncle Ben," Slade smiled, and supplied his own name. They shook hands.

"Now for that hull," Slade said. They approached the mule. Grady managed to loosen the cinch, but one stirrup strap was wedged beneath the carcass.

"Reckon I'll have to cut it," he remarked regretfully, hauling out his knife.

"Hold on a minute," Slade answered. He squatted beside the mule, shoved his hands as far as he could beneath the body. A heave of his broad shoulders, a bunching of great muscles on arms and back and up came the mule's body enough to free the wedged stirrup.

"Good gosh!" exclaimed Uncle Ben as he hauled the saddle free. "Son, I reckon you don't know how strong you are. Wouldn't have believed it if I hadn't seen it!"

Slade smiled and wiped the dust from his hands. "And now I want to have a look at that other carcass," he said as Uncle Ben laid the saddle aside and proceeded to remove the bridle and bit.

With Slade shouldering the saddle, they walked to where the dead man lay, arms wide-flung, glazing eyes glaring up at the sky.

"Got him dead center," Uncle Ben observed as Slade laid down the saddle and gave his attention to the corpse. "Mean-looking sidewinder, ain't he?"

"He is," Slade agreed. He gazed at the dead face a moment, then began turning out the fellow's pockets, discovering nothing he considered significant save a surprisingly large amount of money, which he handed to Uncle Ben.

"Buy yourself another mule," he said.

"Son, I ain't so bad fixed, you keep it," protested Uncle Ben.

"Buy another mule," Slade repeated. "Seeing as they killed yours, it's only fair that they buy you a replacement." Uncle Ben chuckled and pocketed the money. Slade picked up the outlaw's bulky form without apparent effort and placed it at the side of the trail.

"I'll notify the sheriff when we get to town and he can come and look it over, if he wishes to," he said. "I would have liked to get a look at the horse, but it hightailed after the others."

Uncle Ben nodded. Then he turned his faded blue eyes on Slade.

"Son," he said, "as soon as it comes dark, you'd

better fork that big horse of yours and hightail out of this section. Tarp Henry will be out to even this up, and don't you forget it."

"Not much on running," Slade replied cheerfully. "Suppose we head for your cabin. I *could* stand a bite to eat about now, and some coffee will go fine."

Uncle Ben glanced apprehensively along the trail. "Reckon those devils might come back?" he asked.

"Not likely, I'd say," Slade answered. "I've a notion three of them aren't feeling any too good right now. In my opinion they'll keep going until they reach some place where they can get patched up. Let's go." He whistled Shadow, shouldered the saddle and followed Uncle Ben, who walked sturdily despite his limp.

"Sorry to lose old Poky," Uncle Ben remarked regretfully. "I'll have to ride Bat Ears now, the one I left at home. He's okay but hasn't got the savvy Poky had. Razorback Molly there—" he gestured to the pack mule which ambled along beside Shadow—"she's smarter than both of 'em put together. Notice how she dodged aside, just like your cayuse, when I went down. She knew enough to get in the clear."

"A lady is usually the quickest to do the right thing," Slade smiled.

They trudged along and after a while Uncle Ben announced, "Here's the draw. Another half a mile or so and we come to my shack."

They reached the head of the draw with the sun past the zenith. A final fringe of brush and it opened into a wide clearing.

"There she is," said Uncle Ben, "my shack's just ahead, and my mine, if you want to call it that."

Slade paused, and gazed. Directly ahead and a little to the east was what looked like an enormous fortress. It was, in fact, a flat-topped hill or small mountain more than a thousand feet high. Its curving base was formed of sheer black cliffs several hundred feet in height. Above the cliffs rose the steep slope of the rounded, truncated cone, scantily grown with brush. Around the base curved a swift but not very wide stream that plunged into the mouth of a dark and narrow canyon not far distant and around a bulge hidden from view. The mountain cliffs formed the towering south wall of the canyon, with the north wall cresting on a level with the cliff top.

"And you've been mining gold at the base of those cliffs?" he asked.

"That's right," said Uncle Ben. Slade continued to gaze at the cliffs.

5

Not long before the death of his father, which followed shortly after unexpected financial reverses that entailed the loss of the elder Slade's ranch, young Walt had graduated from a famed college of engineering. His intention had been to take a post-graduate course to round out his education and better fit him for the profession he planned to make his life's work. This becoming impossible at the moment, he had lent an attentive ear when Captain Jim McNelty suggested that he join the Rangers for a while and pursue his studies in spare time. The suggestion had proved a good one. Long since, he had gotten more from private study than he could have hoped for from the post-grad and was eminently fitted to enter the profession of engineering.

But often the solution of one problem begets another. Such was the case with Walt Slade. He found that Ranger work had a strong hold on him and he hesitated to sever connections with the illustrious body of law enforcement officers. Why not wait a while! Plenty of time to be an engineer. He'd stick with the Rangers for a little longer. A decision that caused Captain Jim to chuckle.

So now he studied the peculiar formation with a geologist's understanding.

"Uncle Ben," he said. "The gold you have been panning never came from those cliffs. They're lava, not quartz."

Uncle Ben chuckled knowingly. "Guess you're right," he conceded. "Where do you say it came from?"

"Hard to tell," Slade replied. "Lava rock is sometimes a casing over rock of a different nature. In the nature of an icing on a cake, as it were. That's often, in fact, almost always the way with metal-bearing ledges: metal-bearing veins between casings of base rock. Could be here."

"And you'd figure maybe the gold comes from somewhere in behind those cliffs?" said Uncle Ben, cocking an eye at him.

"Not beyond the realm of possibility."

"Perhaps it comes from a long ways up the creek, washed down," suggested Uncle Ben.

"Could be," Slade answered. "We can determine that for sure if you have a specimen or two handy."

"I have," said Uncle Ben. "You 'pear to know considerable about such things."

"Some," Slade conceded, but did not elaborate.

"Right around that little grove over to the left you'll see my shack," said Uncle Ben.

They rounded the grove and Slade gazed with surprise at the big cabin solidly constructed of logs and with a split-pole roof.

"You must have been here quite a while and done a lot of work to build it," he commented, thinking to draw Uncle Ben out, for he knew very well that the cabin was constructed long before the prospector's time. In a way, he succeeded.

"Didn't build it," replied Uncle Ben. "It was built years and years ago, maybe a couple of hundred or so. I found it when I stumbled onto this place. Some funny things in that shack. I'll show you, soon as we put up the critters. I built a snug lean-to in the back. Over there eating grass is my other mule Bat Ears."

As soon as Shadow and the mules were cared for with generous helpin's of oats, Uncle Ben led the way into the cabin, unlocking and swinging back the massive wooden door, which could be barred with iron from the inside.

Slade noticed that the windows were also barred with iron; the shack was a regular fort.

They entered the big living room, which was supplied with home-made chairs and tables, undoubtedly very old but in good repair. Bunks were built along the walls.

"See the loopholes," said Uncle Ben, pointing to narrow slits cut in the logs at intervals. "A couple of fellers could hold this shack against fifty so long as they were not burned out or starved out. Come on."

He ushered Slade into a second room that was

43

evidently a kitchen, as it boasted a wide fireplace and an iron stove.

"Somebody besides the fellers who built the shack brought in that stove," observed Uncle Ben. "It's new compared to the rest of the stuff. The cooking used to be done in the fireplace— hooks and racks there. Now look here."

He flung open a narrow door as he spoke. Slade peered into a third and smaller room with a single window heavily barred. He followed Uncle Ben's pointing finger.

Bolted to the logs were rusty chains ending in iron cuffs. "Leg irons," Slade remarked wonderingly.

"That's right," nodded Uncle Ben. "There were slave fellers kept in this room once upon a time, most likely Indian fellers. You know the old Spaniards caught Indians and made the poor devils do the mining work for them. Soon as I saw those leg irons I was sure for certain there was gold somewhere hereabouts. Now I'll show you those specimens of what I've been panning that you wanted to see."

He took a covered can from a shelf and poured several rough, dull-colored pellets onto the kitchen table. Slade turned one over in his slender fingers. He glanced up to see the old fellow watching him expectantly.

"Well, what do you think of them?" Uncle Ben asked.

"Among other things," Slade replied, "that if these are a fair sample, the gold you've been panning never came down the creek."

"Why do you say that?" questioned Uncle Ben.

"Because the edges are sharp, not rounded and not worn down as they would be had they been washed along by water over a period of years. This stuff came out of the ground quite recently, as you should know."

"Yes, I know it," admitted Uncle Ben. "I wasn't always a miner—started out as a cowhand—but I've learned enough about the business to know that. I wanted to see if you'd agree with me. Nope, that gold never came down the creek. Interesting, don't you think?"

"Extremely interesting," Slade agreed.

"Now I'll get a fire going in the stove and while it gets to burning good I'll show you something else."

The fire was started and a little later the prospector led the way to the edge of the clearing.

"See that big sand bank over there, where the creek bends?" he said. "That's where I've been washing out the same sort of nuggets as I showed you. And it's the only place they can be washed out. I've panned up the creek for miles and never found a trace of color. I've been clean around the darn mountain and there ain't a sign of gold-bearing ledge anywhere. And there ain't a place, incidentally, by way of which a feller could get up the cliffs to the top. A goat couldn't do it, and even a lizard would have sore feet before he made it. Now look up the side of the hill, up above the cliffs."

Slade followed his pointing finger and saw that several hundred feet above the cliff crest was a dark opening. From that opening rushed a small stream of water to come tumbling down the slope and over the cliffs to finally plume for fifty feet in a sheer fall and boil into waters of the creek beneath.

"That's where the gold comes from," Uncle Ben said impressively. "I'll bet my last *peso* on it. That little brook scours it out from somewhere up there. I always get my best pannings a day or so after a hard rain, when the water coming down the hill is sort of muddy and the brook high. You see the brook hits the main creek considerably upstream from the sand bank. The sand bank forms a backwater and the gold settles there. When I first squatted here, the pannings from the bank were mighty rich. After a while, though, they began to taper off and I figured I'd exhausted the pocket. That's when I took to wandering upstream and around the mountain. Was gone nearly a week and came back here a couple of days after a hard rain. Figured I'd give the sand bank another whirl in case I'd missed some color. I was plumb flabbergasted to find the pannings for a while were almost as good as what

46

I got at first. Then I began thinking, and figured the gold came from up there somewhere."

Slade nodded. "I'm inclined to think you're right," he said. "And I'm also inclined to think that somewhere there's a way to the top of the cliffs and no doubt a route by which the source of the gold supply can be reached."

Uncle Ben shook his head vigorously. "There just ain't," he declared.

"How about that canyon over there?" Uncle Ben shook his head again.

"Water fills the canyon from wall to wall, and she runs like a mill race. I was up top the far wall of the canyon, the north wall that's just about level with the cliff top, and the cliffs around the bulge on that side are just the same as they are here, plumb straight-up-and-down."

"When you were traveling around the mountain, did you see any indications of a heavy rock fall or a slide that might have obliterated a way up?" Slade asked. For a third time the prospector shook his head.

"Nary a sign of one," he replied. "I thought of that and looked close. I figure that mountainside and the cliffs are just like they were maybe a million years ago, and that's a lot of time."

"Comparatively short, geologically speaking," Slade differed, with a smile. "But a recent slide would have left plenty of evidence that it happened. So it would appear that if there is a way up, it is obscure and not easy to come by."

"Just the same, you sorta figure there is a way up?" old Ben asked.

"I do," Slade replied.

"Oh, well, maybe there is," conceded Ben. "Okay, let's go rustle that surrounding; I'm beginning to feel the need of it. Fire should be ready for business now."

They cooked and ate an appetizing meal. After which they smoked together in relaxed comfort. Uncle Ben kept glancing at his companion, his grizzled brows drawing together. Slade instinctively sensed that the old fellow had something he rather wanted to tell him and was turning over in his mind whether to or not. Abruptly he appeared to arrive at a decision, and made his approach in an oblique fashion.

"Son," he said, "maybe those hellions didn't figure to kill me with their slugs, and wanted to take me alive. Maybe that's why they downed the mule."

"Possibly," Slade conceded, "but why?"

"Because," old Ben said slowly, "maybe they wanted to know something they maybe think I know."

"Yes?" Slade prompted.

"Maybe they figure I know where the lost Gavilan Mine is."

"The lost Gavilan Mine?" Slade repeated.

"That's right. Ever hear of it?"

48

"I have," Slade replied, "but it is generally assumed that the mine is in the Ashes Mountains spur of the Guadalupes, the Sierra de Cenizas, as Captain de Gavilan called them."

"Uh-huh," said Uncle Ben, "but others will tell you that the mine really was here in these hills. If you've heard the story, you've heard, I reckon, that old Ben Sublett was supposed to get his gold from the lost Gavilan Mine. Sublett brought in plenty from somewhere, nobody ever knew for sure just where, and he never told nobody. I knew Sublett, sorta, when I was younger. We talked together now and then. He sorta cottoned to me, because we were both called Ben, maybe, although his real name was William Colum Sublett. Once when we were talking, I mentioned the Ashes Mountains. Old Sublett sorta twinkled his eyes at me and said, 'Ben, the west Cap Rook hills are a heap closer.' That's all he said, changed the subject right off, and I didn't ask him what he meant. Fact was I wasn't much interested; I was punchin' cows then. Later, when I started out prospecting, what he said came back to me and got me to wondering. Wondering if Sublett was dropping me a little hint as to the real place to look. The notion sorta got hold of me and I started looking. Finally stumbled on this place, as I said before, and figured mighty fast, after I saw how old the cabin was and saw those leg irons, that some Spaniards were here first. Maybe de Gavilan."

Ben paused to light his pipe, and then continued—"And I'll tell you something else. I got a look at some of the gold Ben Sublett brought in—he lived in Odessa not so far over to the west of here—and the nuggets he brought in looked exactly like those in that can on the shelf. Looked like they'd laid out in the open air for quite a spell. All the gold he brought in looked like that, I understand. It sure wasn't recent dug out of the ground or washed from a creek. I'm plumb sure the nuggets in that can are just the same as those Sublett brought in."

"Could be," Slade agreed. "And I'm willing to concede that the nuggets you showed me have been exposed to the open air for quite a period of time. Could be just coincidence, of course, but it's interesting. Perhaps you have stumbled into the neighborhood of the Gavilan Mine. If so," he added with a smile, "if you can manage to locate a way up the cliffs, you'll quite likely find where the nuggets came from."

"That's just what I believe," Uncle Ben said seriously. "Say, why don't you stay here and help me look for it. You got young eyes and mighty sharp ones. Maybe you'll see something I've overlooked. Anyhow, you can pan out enough gold from the sand bank to make it worth your while more than you can tie onto chambermaiding cows."

"Thanks for the offer, Uncle Ben," Slade

replied. "But I've got to get back to town tomorrow. I'll promise you one thing, though," he said, the sudden decision based on something that had abruptly clicked in his alert mind, "I'll drop over here every now and then for a look around, so long as I'm in the section. Tomorrow I'll ride to Signal with you, just in case."

"Uh-huh, just in case those hellions take a notion to make another try," said Uncle Ben, with perfect understanding. "With you along I hope they do try it, and I hope Tarp Henry himself is along. Then we won't have to bother about that pest any more."

6

Slade slept soundly on one of the bunks and daybreak found him and the prospector astir. After a hearty breakfast they set out for town, Uncle Ben riding Bat Ears and leading the pack-saddled Razorback Molly. Tarp Henry failed to oblige by putting in an appearance and they reached Signal without incident.

First thing, Uncle Ben deposited his gold in the bank, where it was weighed and a receipt given him. The bank would send it to a Government Assay Office where it would be purchased and the money remitted to his account. Next, Shadow and the mules were stabled.

"And now for a couple of snorts and a surroundin'," said Uncle Ben. "I usually eat at Wingless Angel's place, the Hogwaller."

"I'll walk over there with you," Slade agreed. "Sheriff Chester may be there. Understand he hangs out there a good deal of his spare time."

When they entered the Hogwaller, they were both warmly greeted by Wingless Angel, who conducted them to a table. Uncle Ben sat down. Slade remained standing, glancing about.

"Don't see Chester," he said. "I'll drop over to his office. Be back shortly."

Ben Grady was well known in Signal and a crowd soon gathered around him.

"Brought in another poke, eh?" somebody remarked. "Have a good trip?"

"Uh-huh, a sorta exciting one, but I made it," returned Grady.

"You were lucky you weren't robbed and murdered," said a frowsy-looking individual who had only one eye. "That big hellion who walked in with you is El Halcón the outlaw."

Uncle Ben glared at him, and his bewhiskered face flushed a dark red. He reached down, hauled out the horse pistol, cocked it and banged the table with the barrel. There was a frantic scramble to get out of line with the nail-keg muzzle.

"Gents!" roared Uncle Ben, "I'm plumb in the notion of plugging somebody. I ain't saying who, but I betcha I shoot his other eye out!"

The one-eyed man was half under a table. "Hold it, Ben, hold it!" he squalled. "I didn't mean nothin'. I was just telling you what folks say."

"Say and be damned to them!" growled Grady, waving the horse pistol. "And let me say something to *you,* and to the rest of you! I packed in a poke with nearly a thousand dollars' worth of gold in it, and that feller Slade knew I was packing it. And he rode along with me to make sure I'd get in safe. And I felt as safe as if a whole dadblamed troop of Jim McNelty's Rangers were alongside of me. And let me tell you what else he did."

Then followed a graphic account of the brush with the outlaws, stressing the part Slade had played in the ruckus.

"Whe-e-ew!" somebody exclaimed. "And he killed two of Tarp Henry's men in here just the other night! Henry will sure be looking for him."

"Uh-huh, and I've a notion he'll be looking for Henry," predicted Uncle Ben. "And I got another notion. A notion that we won't be pestered with that sidewinder much longer. And if anybody has something else to say about Slade, this is just the time to say it; here he comes in the door right now."

What followed was a profound and eloquent silence.

"Chester wasn't in," Slade said as he sat down and beckoned a waiter, the crowd having discreetly melted away. "I left word that he could find us here for a while."

"Okay," said Uncle Ben, "let's eat. I waited for you. Hello, here comes Tom Bowles, the coroner, a fine feller. Have you met him?"

"Known him for quite a while," Slade replied.

"Howdy, Walt?" said Bowles, as he drew near. "Sorry to find you in such bad company. This old coot is fuller of fleas than a stray dog."

"Better than to be always full of bug juice, like some folks I could mention," retorted Uncle Ben. "Take a load off your feet, Tom, and have a snort."

"Don't mind if I do," said Bowles, drawing up a chair. "Well, what's new?"

Uncle Ben repeated his version of the run-in with Tarp Henry's owlhoots. Bowles did not appear overly impressed.

"You must be slipping, Walt," he said. "Downed only one of them? Time was when you would have done for all five with two shots. Yep, you're slipping. Oh, well, old age creeps up on all of us. Fill 'em up again, waiter!"

Before they finished eating, Sheriff Chester arrived and also drew up a chair.

"Well, well!" said Uncle Ben. "The coroner and the sheriff! Now if Doc McChesney will just show up, all we'll need is the undertaker."

"You've got a fair substitute for him right alongside you," snorted the sheriff. "Well, Slade, how many have you killed today?"

"None so far, and only one yesterday," Slade smiled reply.

"What's that!" exploded the sheriff, sitting bolt upright. Uncle Ben again repeated his story. The sheriff sighed dismally.

"I might have known it," he said. "Slade, I don't know whether what folks say about you is true or not, though I admit, I can't find any reward notices on you, but one thing is sure for certain; trouble just follows you around."

"Trouble for the wrong sort," observed Tom Bowles. "Saves you a chore."

"But why does he have to kill people so far off?" wailed the sheriff. "Now I've got to ride way over there to fetch in a worthless carcass."

"Good for you," said Uncle Ben. "May shake off some of the tallow; you could lose about a ton and not miss it."

"Better to be fat and sleep well with a good conscience than to be gaunt as a gutted sparrow like you, you ganglin' string bean," retorted the sheriff.

"Uh-huh, you sleep all right," agreed Uncle Ben. "I been waiting for I don't know how long for you to wake up, but I'm just about ready to give up hope. Have a drink, Chet."

The sheriff swallowed his drink and stood up. "I'll have to be moving," he said. "It'll be way past dark by the time I get back, as is. Something over a mile this side of the draw you said, Ben? All right, I'll find the varmint, if the coyotes don't get to him first."

"He was still in one piece when we passed by this morning," returned Uncle Ben. "Be seeing you."

"And, Slade, if you don't think I'm presuming, I'll give you a mite of good advice," Chester added. "Don't be riding around alone. Tarp Henry is no pushover, and he'll be out to get you."

"Thank you, Sheriff," the Ranger replied. "I'll try and be careful."

"And now I've got to mosey out and corral

a sack full of provisions and stuff," said Uncle Ben. "Meet you fellers here after dark."

"And I've got to get back to my shop," said Bowles. "So long, Walt, be seeing you. Come on, Ben, I suppose you'll be stopping at my place."

They left the saloon together. Slade ordered more coffee, rolled a cigarette, relaxed comfortably in his chair and gave himself over to thought.

Was it possible, he wondered, that old Ben had really stumbled onto the general location of the famed Gavilan Mine. In the face of the general consensus that the mine was really hidden somewhere in the Ashes Mountains country, it didn't seem reasonable; but general opinion could be wrong. In the mountains to the west, gold was found. Also, silver, lead and copper. But once again the general consensus maintained that there was no gold worth prospecting for in the Cap Rock hills here to the east of the mountains. However, Ben Grady had conclusively proven there *was* gold in the hills, in sufficient quantity to justify prospecting for it. And Slade recalled a prospector's saying, "Gold is where you find it." Which had more than once confounded popular beliefs. There might well be a mine somewhere in the vicinity of the sand bank from which Grady panned gold.

It was not necessarily the legendary Gavilan Mine. In fact, there had never been any proof positive that Sublett ever discovered the Gavilan Mine, although he led people to believe he did. That might well be in the nature of a subterfuge employed to keep folks away from his real discovery. His mine could easily be elsewhere. The Spanish invaders, hundreds of years before, had mined gold in unexpected places and sometimes had had to abandon their workings because of Indian uprisings. Naturally they kept their location a secret, hoping one day to return and resume operations. Could be the case here.

To a casual observer, it might have seemed that Slade's interest in the mine was a bit off-trail; he had been sent to the Signal country to run down an outlaw band, not to search for mythical gold diggings. The truth was quite the contrary. He was playing a hunch based on the idea that had occurred to him the night before. Ben Grady appeared to be of the opinion that Tarp Henry was interested in his search for the mine. If so and the outlaw leader concluded that Grady had actually discovered the mystery mine, he would very probably make a try for it. Which meant he would come to Ben Grady. And, incidentally, he might very well also come to El Halcón. Which Slade hoped he would do. He didn't know where to look for Tarp Henry and he had no idea, so far, who Tarp Henry might really be, although he was of the opinion, based on past experience, that when and if Henry's identity were revealed, a lot of folks might be in for something of a surprise. So Ben Grady and the legendary mine were something in the nature of bait and if Henry swallowed it, he could possibly find himself neatly on the hook.

There was only one flaw to the plan. If it worked, it would lay old Ben Grady open to grave personal danger, which Slade knew he must prevent at all costs. It was not unlikely that Grady was already in danger; that he would endeavor to minimize. Wingless Angel, who habitually used a bull bellow for ordinary conversation, inadvertently provided him with an opportunity. He strolled over to the table and inquired,

"Well, has old Ben found his lost Gavilan Mine?"

Purposely raising his voice so that it would carry clearly to the bar, Slade replied, "No, he hasn't found it yet, but he's looking, and I consider it not beyond the realm of possibility that he will eventually find it."

Now! If one of Tarp Henry's minions happened to be in the saloon, which Slade considered not unlikely, the Hogwaller being a gathering place for all sorts and prime for obtaining information relative to what was going on in the section, he would undoubtedly carry the word to his boss. Which would mean that while a watch would probably be kept on Uncle Ben he wouldn't be molested until Henry felt sure he'd actually discovered the mine. Or so Slade hoped. Later, he and old Ben might be able to formulate a scheme that would work. Worth trying, anyhow.

He had noted with satisfaction that when he answered Wingless Angel's question, a couple of men at the bar who had been talking together turned quickly to glance fleetingly in his direction and immediately turned back again, as if the movement were involuntary.

Might mean nothing, of course, their glances motivated only by idle curiosity. Then again it might mean something; they had appeared almost startled.

He studied the pair. They were dressed as cowhands but he shrewdly suspected that there were no recent marks of rope or branding iron on their hands. They were hard-looking individuals who needed a shave and wore their holsters low and slightly to the front. He would recognize them if he saw them again. A few moments later they walked out; they did not again glance in his direction.

Wingless approached the table again. "Pretty near forgot it," he remarked, "but Val Parker was in last night and asked for you. Said he'd be back tonight. 'Peared anxious to see you. He's a rowdy young feller, but I don't think there's any real harm in him; just rambunctious and full of the Old Harry, like lots of fellers his age. Craves excitement." Slade nodded; he had formed something of the same opinion of Parker.

"I expect to meet Uncle Ben and Tom Bowles here later," he said. "You might mention it to Parker if he happens to show up before then."

"I'll do that," Wingless promised. "Doc McChesney was in, too, and wanted to know what the blankety-blank-blank became of you. Said you slid out of his place sometime before he woke up. I told him I hadn't seen you all day. He said he was going home and sharpen up his tools; said he figured he'd be needing them."

"I'm afraid not," Slade smiled. "I don't think those punctured gents Uncle Ben told you about would show up here for treatment."

"A notion you got the right of it," nodded Wingless. "Chances are they hightailed clean to Odessa or someplace to get patched up. Chances are they'd figure it was sorta unhealthy around here. Be seeing you."

Shortly afterward, Slade left the Hogwaller. First he repaired to Doc McChesney's place to reassure the physician, who evidently was worried about him. Doc demanded to know what he had been up to and Slade regaled him with an account of his adventures of the day before.

"Glad you happened along when you did," said Doc. "Ben Grady's okay; a fine feller. Sorta loco, I reckon, like all prospectors and desert rats, but he's all right. Been browsin' around in the hills for quite a spell now. Didn't do much good until

61

a coupla months back, when he began bringing in metal regular. Everybody was glad he'd made a strike at last. Keeps saying he's going to hit it big before he's finished, but they all say that. Mostly sheep dip. Now and then, though, some of them do hit the jackpot, like Ben Sublett did, or Ed Schefflin over at Tombstone, Arizona. Nope, you never can tell. Thought once or twice I'd sorta like to give it a try myself, but never did. Always too busy mining lead out of jiggers to have a chance to try my hand at gold."

"I expect your lead mining will prove more lucrative in the end," Slade said, with a smile. "That's one claim that never peters out."

"Especially with hellions like El Halcón around," Doc agreed. "Why didn't you herd those three punctured gents here for me to work over?"

"I fear only an extra long-winded flash of lightning could have caught up with them, the way they hightailed after Ben blew half of one's face off with that wheelless cannon he packs," Slade replied. "I promised Bowles and Uncle Ben I'd meet them at the Hogwaller shortly after dark. Perhaps you can find time to drop over."

"I'll be there," McChesney replied. "We'll eat together; get tired of my own cooking now and then."

"Just the same, you throw together a prime surrounding," Slade observed.

"Anyhow, I don't have to worry about being

poisoned, as I would if some female was doing it for me," grunted Doc, a confirmed bachelor of sixty-eight.

Slade laughed and went out for a walk around town.

7

He found the town interesting and predicted it would grow. Once it had marked a stopping point on the Comanche war trail, which swept down from the High Plains and curved southwest to follow a line of watering places to the Comanche Crossing deep in the Big Bend. Later, it was a watering place where buffalo hunters and bone gatherers erected their hide and wood huts. Now the surrounding territory was largely cattle country, but the plow of the farmer was turning over more and more nearby square miles of rangeland and agriculture could not be ruled out. Cotton and grains grew well except in periods of drought. For the present, however, the cow was holding its own. Also, in addition to what might be found in the Cap Rock hills, the soil of yellow bluffs northeast of the town assayed placer gold in quantities to make working profitable. In years to come, not too far away, Signal would become much more cosmopolitan.

At the present, however, it was a typical cow-town, peaceful enough most of the time but capable of blowing sky high at any moment.

It was shortly after sunset, with the dark closing down, when Slade found himself in the eastern portion of the town, which was the Mexican quarter. He strolled around a bit and several times was joyously greeted as El Halcón. Finally he headed back to the business section. It was now full dark and the streets, given over mostly to warehouses, were poorly lighted.

But there was light enough for Slade to spot the two men sauntering along some distance behind him. He waited until they were passing under a street light so he could shoot a swift glance sideways over his shoulder. He recognized the two individuals who had appeared to take an interest in him while he and Wingless Angel were discussing the possibility of Uncle Ben's discovering the Gavilan Mine.

Now what? he wondered. They appeared to be keeping their distance. It might mean nothing, of course; they, too, might just be taking an aimless stroll. But there was a purposeful appearance about them that caused the Ranger to doubt that convenient explanation. He quickened his pace a little, his eyes slanting across the street to where the unlighted windows of a warehouse provided a fair imitation of a mirror. Instantly he became very much on the alert; the pair had also speeded up. He resumed his former gait. The pair did likewise.

Slade was a bit puzzled. Didn't seem likely that they would try a dry-gulching here on an open street. It would be rather too risky, even with the odds two to one. So what did they have in mind, if anything?

Then abruptly he understood. Coming along the street toward him was another pair, hatbrims drawn low, hands close to their holsters. So that was it! Catch him in a deadly crossfire. His mind worked at racing speed. Two to one and the odds were not too heavy. Four to one was a mite lopsided. But what still puzzled him was the fact that the pair behind were not closing in; they were still a bit too far for anything like accurate sixgun work, and he didn't see any rifles.

Directly ahead, a dark and narrow alley opened onto the street. Slade walked along unconcernedly until he reached the alley. With a sideways leap he whisked into it and raced ahead, listening for accelerated footsteps behind him.

But his mind was still working fast and he was far from satisfied with developments. It looked like the quartette had deliberately herded him into the alley. He slowed his pace, one hand brushing the wall of the buildings which flanked the alley. It was very dark, but ahead, now not more than a score of yards distant, was the other end of it, which he knew by the fact that the light was brighter there. Behind him, still some distance behind, sounded the padding of stealthy feet.

Abruptly his hand brushing the wall encountered nothing but emptiness for a few feet. It was an opening between two buildings. He slid into the crack, which was barely wide enough to accommodate his body. As he did so, he stepped on a round boulder that rolled slightly under his foot and very nearly caused him to stumble. He caught his balance without making a racket, however, and halted, shifting his foot away from the stone. Suddenly he had an idea as to how it might be put to use. He stooped, groped it into his hand and straightened up. It was a sizeable rock a couple of pounds in weight. Edging back a step he found he could go no farther because of the narrowing of the opening. Tense, motionless, he waited as the soft tread of advancing feet grew more distinct.

A clump of shadows loomed amid the other shadows. Slade held his breath, one hand touching his gun butt, the other poising the stone. To his keen ears came a low mutter: "Easy! If we don't get him, the boys at the other end will. Easy! He's dangerous. If you hear anything, shoot."

The shadows drifted past, slowly. Careful to make no sound, Slade eased out of the crack. He waited a moment longer, then hurled the stone up the alley, well above the heads of the four men. Whirling, he raced back down the alley the way he had come.

The stone hit the ground with a thump and bounded along, a very fair imitation of running feet. Instantly the alley volcanoed action. At the far mouth, guns boomed. Guns down the alley joined in. There was a howl of pain, yells, curses, another howl. More shooting! More swearing! A wild babble of bellowing voices! Slade shook with laughter as he whisked out of the alley and sped along the street. The bounding stone had fooled both groups and they were gunning each other. He crossed a side street, whipped around a corner, another, and slowed up. Directly ahead was the business section of the town. There were lights, people moving about. Slade sauntered along, still chuckling. He reached the Hogwaller and entered, found a vacant table and sat down, still breathing a bit hard.

Wingless Angel strolled over and plumped into a vacant chair.

"Well, how goes it?" he asked.

"Fine as frog hair," Slade replied. "I promised Bowles and Doc McChesney and Uncle Ben that I'd join them here for dinner. Guess I'm a little ahead of time; I'll have some coffee while waiting for them."

Wingless beckoned a waiter, who brought the coffee. Slade was sipping it when Sheriff Chester stalked in glowering about. He spotted Slade and approached purposefully, still glowering.

"Where'd you come from?" he asked abruptly.

"Been here all evening," Wingless volunteered before Slade could speak.

"That's funny," snorted the sheriff. "How come there's a ruckus and him not in the middle of it?"

"What you mean, Chet?" asked Wingless.

"There was one devil of a row over on Sherman Street just a little bit ago," said Chester. "Folks said there was shooting and yelling and cussing like all blazes. Said it sounded like somebody got nicked. I hustled over there but couldn't find anything. Must have been a good one, though. Reckon the bodies were packed off before I got there."

"Just a bunch of cowhands shootin' out the stars, I reckon," said Wingless. "Getting to be like the old days, eh, Chet?"

"Yes, but then you usually knew who was kicking up the shindig, now you don't know nothin'," grumbled the sheriff. "Enough to drive a man loco." He favored Slade with an injured glance.

"Wherever you show up, trouble starts bustin' loose," he said. "Blazes! here come those other three horned toads! Lemme outta here!"

He suited the action to the word and stalked out, replying gruffly to the greetings of Bowles, McChesney and Uncle Ben, who had just entered. They immediately made their way to Slade's table and sat down.

"And now, Walt, seeing as we've gotten rid of that minion of the law, suppose you tell us what did happen," suggested Wingless.

Slade told them, in detail. Wingless chuckled. Uncle Ben clucked and shook his grizzled head. Bowles swore.

"I'm losing out on too much business," complained Doc McChesney.

"Just the same, it's no joke," growled Bowles. "Henry's hellions are after him hot and heavy."

"Well, so long as they spend their time throwing lead at one another, there's not too much to worry about," Slade said cheerfully.

"Yes, but it may be different next time," was Bowles's gloomy retort.

"My money's on Slade," declared Wingless. "He'll give them their come-uppance, no doubt in my mind as to that. What do you say, Uncle Ben?"

"Well, after watching him send a whole flock of 'em skalleyhootin', I'm plumb inclined to agree with you," replied the prospector.

"Don't worry about him," said Doc. "Some particular devil looks after his own."

Bowles still did not look convinced, but he subsided after a grumble or two.

"Let's eat," said Doc. "Then we'll all have a few drinks and sorta get into the swing of things."

Nobody objected to that. Wingless waved to a waiter and they gave their orders.

"I'm having a bite with you," announced Wingless. "Been too busy to eat, since I came in; business is good."

"Too darn good," grunted Bowles, still pessimistic. "Betcha something busts loose before the night's over."

"Stop croaking, Tom," advised Doc. "All's well with the world."

After a hearty meal washed down by numerous cups of coffee, even Bowles developed a better frame of mind. A couple of snorts to hold down the chuck and he became quite cheerful.

"Hello!" he exclaimed suddenly. "Here comes Val Parker. What the devil happened to him?"

8

Parker had paused just inside the swinging doors and was sweeping the room with a searching gaze. His hat was tipped back and a reddened handkerchief was tied around his head. He spotted the occupants of the table and approached.

"Sit down," invited Bowles. "What happened to *you?*"

Parker drew up a chair. "Bit myself," he replied cheerfully. Bowles cocked an eye at the bandaged forehead. "Way up there?"

"Well, I could have stood on a chair, couldn't I?" Parker retorted. He grinned.

"Fellers," he said, "I don't know for sure just what happened to me or why. I was riding where the trail skirts that brush-covered ridge about five miles out of town. Was close to sunset. Well, all of a sudden something smacked me, hard. Knocked me out of the hull and half silly for a moment. I didn't know what had hit me, but as I went down, I saw smoke drift up from the crest of the ridge. Took me two or three minutes to get my scrambled senses back together and when I was able to stand up, I didn't see anything up there. Somebody threw a slug at me, but who or why I haven't the slightest notion. I've had rows

72

with a few fellers, but none of them were the sort that would go in for a dry-gulching or shooting one in the back. I can't understand it."

"You've been sounding off about the Henry bunch, haven't you?" said Bowles.

"Well, I have a habit of speaking my mind, and doubtless some of the remarks I've made about those hellions might be considered derogatory," Parker admitted.

"That's it, I'd say, the blankety-blank-blanks!" swore Bowles.

"Better let me have a look at that head," Doc McChesney broke in. "Could be a fracture, or concussion."

"I think we can dismiss the likelihood of fracture," Parker replied. "There is no throbbing pain, and the wound bled quite freely. Concussion, of course, is a different matter and can lead to serious complications. I don't think there is concussion, but of course the diagnosis of a layman can be erroneous. Guess you had better have a look at it."

He undid the handkerchief as he spoke, revealing a ragged tear just above the left temple.

Doc grunted. Bowles and Uncle Ben and Wingless said things that were not nice. Slade sat silent, regarding Parker intently.

With his gnarled but sensitive old fingers, Doc probed the locality of the wound, examined the cut carefully.

"Guess you're right," he said. "There is no evidence of concussion, so far as I can see. Wingless, get your bandages and salve and a little warm water and we'll patch him up."

The medicants were quickly forthcoming and Doc soon had everything under control. When he had finished, Parker pressed a bill into his hand. Doc glanced at it and started to protest.

"A doctor is entitled to adequate compensation for his work," Parker interrupted. "Even though he doesn't find much to do, one's peace of mind is worth something. Don't you think so, Mr. Slade?"

"I do," the Ranger agreed.

"Well, I'm going to stable my horse before I eat," Parker said. "Come and take a look at him, Mr. Slade; I've a notion you'll like him. We'll be back in a jiffy, folks."

Realizing perfectly well that Parker was anxious to get him alone, Slade followed him to the hitchrack, where Parker pointed out a tall black horse with good lines.

"He's not the equal of your black, but he's not bad," said Parker. "In fact, at a distance of say four hundred yards, he could easily be taken for your horse, don't you think?"

"I'm inclined to agree with you," Slade replied.

"I'm not quite as tall as you—lack a couple of inches, I'd say—but I'm not short, and I'm built rather husky, as you are," Parker continued.

"Also, I have dark hair, not quite as black as yours, but near enough."

Slade nodded; he had a very good notion as to what was coming.

"The other night," Parker resumed, "after I'd expressed the wish that you would sign up with me for a job of riding, I went back to the bar and mentioned the matter to a couple of my boys there, expressing the hope that you would sign up and that probably you would do so. Well, I've a notion the wrong pair of ears were listening and somebody jumped to a conclusion. Were you by any chance absent from town yesterday?" Slade nodded again.

"And doubtless somebody who had been keeping tabs on you and lost track of you decided that you had ridden to my place. So, Mr. Slade, my deduction is that the slug which would have drilled me dead center had I not happened to turn in the saddle just then was meant for you."

"You may have the right of it," Slade conceded.

"Which means," Parker concluded soberly, "that you will be in constant danger so long as you remain in the section."

"Possibly," Slade admitted.

"Well, if you decide to remain, the offer of a job still stands," Parker said. Suddenly he grinned, and his heavy face seemed almost boyish.

"But I think," he said, "that in the future I'll ride a white horse." They laughed together.

"I'm going to stable my critter and then have something to eat," Parker said. "Be seeing you."

Slade walked back to the Hogwaller in a very thoughtful frame of mind. Parker's explanation of how he had received the gunshot wound had been plausible, his deduction as to why he had received it not illogical. The latter, Slade felt, denoted a quick mind and a somewhat unusual ability to analyze a situation. But the possibility of a very vivid imagination was not to be altogether ruled out. Slade wondered if Parker had discarded a handkerchief with which he had first bandaged his wound and replaced it with another before reaching town. For it had seemed to the Ranger's keen eyes that the blood stains were unduly fresh after a five-mile ride.

"Well, what did you think of the cayuse?" Bowles asked when Slade resumed his seat at the table.

"A very nice horse, he has reason to be proud of him," Slade replied.

"Parker is rated a good judge of horse flesh," remarked Wingless. "No snide when it comes to judging cows, too; he's got the best of improved stock on his place. He's had plenty of experience with cattle."

"I wouldn't put his cows ahead of Allen Curtis's," observed Bowles. "About on a par, I'd say."

"They're both cowmen, no doubt as to that," said McChesney. "Difference is, Curtis is a courteous gentleman, while Parker is a good deal of a roughneck. What do you think, Walt?"

"That surface indications can sometimes be deceptive," Slade answered.

"Pinning you down to a positive opinion is like trying to hold water in a clenched fist," grumbled Doc.

"It is best not to until one is in a position to do so as a deliberate expression of his mature views," Slade returned smilingly.

"One thing you and Parker have in common," remarked Bowles. "You both talk like a dictionary; only Parker sort of garbles it at times."

Slade smiled again, and nodded. With the latter part of Bowles's statement he was in accord. Parker's mode of expressing himself was a rather startling potpourri of rangeland colloquialism and correct, almost stilted phraseology. Because of which, El Halcón was forming a definite opinion as to Val Parker's antecedents.

Parker returned a few minutes later. He waved to Slade and joined three of his hands who were eating at a table on the other side of the room.

"He may be a roughneck, but his boys sure swear by him," commented Wingless. "They'll back him up in anything, no questions asked."

"It's a close-knit outfit, all right," observed

77

Bowles. "Did you ever notice, they don't mix much; keep mostly to themselves. I've a notion most of 'em aren't Texans. I've noticed two or three of them riding center-fire saddles with *látigos* instead of a trunk strap."

"California or Arizona rig," Slade commented. "Those single-cinch saddles cut a poor horse in two if they're cinched up tight."

Bowles and Wingless, both former cowhands, nodded agreement.

Quite a few drinks had been imbibed by then and the group at the table was growing animated. Doc McChesney was full of interesting anecdotes based on his professional experiences, while old Ben told startling stories dealing with the idiosyncrasies of prospectors and desert rats. Bowles and Wingless were also raconteurs, and the latter was racy.

Slade, however, sat mostly silent, for his thoughts were elsewhere. From where he sat he had a good view of the table occupied by Val Parker and his hands and was able to study the ranch-owner in a period of relaxation. Parker, he noted, drank sparingly and appeared to be little affected by what he did drink. And he appeared as preoccupied as Slade himself. Slade felt that the man had something on his mind that was giving him concern. It was something beyond his worries in relation to that head wound, Slade was sure. Just what, he wondered.

All in all, Val Parker was something of an enigma, and as such, was of particular interest to El Halcón.

Bowles suddenly uttered an exclamation, "Looks like the clans are gathering; here comes Al Curtis."

Slade had already noticed the entrance of the handsome, debonair owner of the Forked S. With him were two companions in rangeland garb, doubtless a couple of his riders.

Curtis waved to Bowles, then he and his riders took a table not far from the one occupied by Val Parker and his hands. Slade noted that Curtis shot a swift glance at Parker, then to all appearances ignored him. As for Parker, he paid not the slightest attention to the other, although it seemed to El Halcón that he stiffened the merest trifle as Curtis brushed past him. He recalled Tom Bowles mentioning that the two owners, while next-door neighbors, did not get along any too well. He caught Bowles's attention and asked, "What was the trouble between Curtis and Parker?"

"A row over what often causes trouble in dry country, water," Bowles replied. "Curtis diverted a small stream that used to run across Parker's holding. Parker didn't like it and told Curtis so, in no uncertain terms; but there wasn't anything much he could do about it. Curtis said he was within his legal rights, which he was; the stream had its source on his holding, and of course it wasn't navigable."

"Damage Parker's property much?"

Bowles shook his head. "No, but he had to run ditches and dig waterholes because of it, which didn't sit very well. He has good water on his land, but that stream reached a section of it that was dry otherwise."

Slade nodded his understanding. Curtis was within his legal rights, certainly, but it wasn't a very considerate thing to do. He asked another question, "Curtis need that water badly?"

Bowles again shook his head. "Nope, he could have gotten along very well without it," he answered. "But it provided a convenience and saved him from running ditches. I've a notion Parker rubbed him the wrong way over something. As I said, Parker is quick-tempered and inclined to be quarrelsome, while Curtis is just the opposite. Would have been better if there was another spread between their holdings. Oh, well, takes all sorts to make a world."

"And the world needs most sorts, even though sometimes we wonder why," Slade remarked.

Doc McChesney glanced at the clock. "I'm going to bed," he suddenly announced. "What about you, Walt?"

"A good notion," Slade replied. "Me, too. Heading back for your claim in the morning, Uncle Ben?"

"Yep, guess I'd better," Grady answered. "Can't afford to loaf too long."

"I'll be riding over to visit you soon," Slade said. "Good night, Tom."

As he and Doc left the table, Val Parker turned and beckoned him.

"How about riding out to my place in the morning?" Parker suggested when Slade drew near. "The boys are heading back tonight, but I've got to stay over to attend to a couple of matters. Okay?"

"Not a bad idea," Slade accepted. "I'll meet you here."

As he spoke he noted Allen Curtis flicker a glance in his direction; he had evidently overheard the conversation, and quite likely did not approve of Slade's choice of associates.

9

After a good night's rest and a leisurely breakfast prepared by Doc McChesney, Slade repaired to the Hogwaller to wait for Parker to put in an appearance.

He didn't have to wait long; very shortly the Bar Cross owner entered, glanced around and spotted him.

"One snort to hold my breakfast down and I'm all set," he said.

He downed the snort with dispatch, wiped his lips with the back of his hand and said, "Let's go."

They got the rigs on their horses and headed east. Soon they left the straggle of hills and were riding across the open prairie.

"It's all good range," Parker remarked. "To the north of my holding is Allen Curtis's Forked S. To the south is the Lazy JL owned by the youngest son of Lord Ragnal of England. He knows about as much about the cattle business as I know about reading hieroglyphics, even when he's sober enough to see anything as small as a cow, which isn't often. But he has a good range boss and makes out.

"Speaking of range bosses," he added, "that's what I'll have in line for you if you see fit to sign on with me. I've been handling that chore myself, but with a multiplicity of other duties, it becomes irksome, especially as I'm hoping to expand a bit. I'm pretty sure the Lazy JL is going to be put up for sale soon. Young Ragnal doesn't like this isolation and longs for the cities. If he decides to sell, I'll get first whack; he's promised me that, and no matter what else he may be, he's a man of his word. So it really is essential for me to acquire an assistant on whom I can depend."

"I appreciate your confidence, Mr. Parker," Slade replied, refraining from committing himself one way or the other.

"I'm confident it isn't misplaced," said Parker. "Oh, call me Val; you make me feel ancient, and really I'm not much older than yourself, although the lines of dissipation which you lack make me appear so."

Slade glanced at the rancher's rugged, deeply bronzed face and stalwart form and smiled.

"Okay, Val, we'll talk things over later," he said.

Parker nodded and pointed ahead. "There's the ridge from which that sidewinder took a shot at me," he observed. "It curves around to the trail a mile from here and the brush is thin. But another half mile farther on the trail edges away from it and it's heavily grown with chaparral that provides good concealment for a dry-gulcher."

Slade nodded, and studied the ridge, the near

terminus of which did edge close to the trail.

"I'd like to ride up there," he remarked. "Shouldn't be difficult to reach the crest by way of this end where the growth is scant. Might be able to pick up that hellion's trail and perhaps get a notion where he came from."

"By gosh! that's right," agreed Parker. "We'll do it."

When they reached the west foot of the brush-grown ridge, Parker immediately forged ahead. Slade did not fail to notice that. He contemplated the rancher's broad back. Parker might not know it, but the authenticity of his story of the night before was soon to be verified or disproven. Had a dry-gulcher really been holed up on the ridge, the keen eyes of El Halcón would quickly discover evidence of the fact.

They made their way to the crest of the ridge without difficulty. On the crest, however, it was a different matter. But the horses forced their way through the thorny tangle without too much protest. Every now and then the growth would thin a little and Slade was able to get a view ahead. They were perhaps a fifth of a mile from where Parker said the dry-gulcher had been holed up when Slade suddenly exclaimed, "Hold it!"

Parker obediently reined in, glancing inquiringly at his companion.

Slade's gaze was fixed ahead, to where the growth was thicker and taller. He stared intently for several moments before voicing an explanation.

"See that blue jay whirling and darting over that thicket?" he said. "I've a notion that from where old fuss-and-feathers is cutting up there is an excellent view of the trail about four hundred yards' distant, easy rifle shooting range."

"Why—why, I've a notion you're right," Parker agreed.

"And for some reason that sky-colored coot is raising the devil," Slade commented. "Now just why is he doing that?"

"Maybe a snake fooling around his nest, or a coyote underneath it," Parker guessed. Slade shook his head.

"To a coyote, he'd pay no mind—coyotes are not interested in blue jay eggs or baby blue jays—and a snake he'd peck the eyes out of in no time, even admitting that a snake would be fool enough to try conclusions with a blue jay," Slade differed. "But something over there has got him badly worked up, something he doesn't understand and in consequence fears."

"What?" wondered Parker. Slade replied obliquely, "A blue jay does not like for a human to be close to its nest!"

Parker stared. "You mean that hellion who took the shot at me may be holed up there waiting for another chance?"

"Not beyond the realm of possibility, he or

another of similar ilk," Slade replied. "Anyhow, I intend to find out before we ride any farther and make setting quail of ourselves." He swung down from the saddle as he spoke; Parker also started to dismount.

"I'll go with you," he said.

"You'll stay right where you are, and make sure your horse keeps quiet," Slade ordered.

"But—" Parker began.

"Do as I tell you," Slade snapped, letting the full force of his cold gray eyes rest on the rancher's face.

Parker subsided, to mutterings. Slade, with a glance around, melted into the growth so silently and swiftly that the rancher did not hear and hardly saw him go; one second he was, the next he just wasn't. Parker shook his head and muttered to the horses, "I've heard Indians could do it, but never thought to see or, rather, not see a white man do it."

Still without making the slightest sound, Slade wormed his way swiftly through the thorny chaparral. He had covered two-thirds of the distance to where the blue jay was cutting up before he slowed. Then he proceeded with the utmost caution, pausing from time to time to peer and listen.

Yard by stealthy yard he crept ahead, estimating the distance covered. The angry blue jay provided a dependable guide. A few minutes later

Slade saw the cerulean flicker of his wings as he flashed through the upper growth.

Another moment and he saw the dry-gulcher, crouching at the outer fringe of the brush, eyes fixed on the trail below, ready rifle to the front.

A flame of wrath enveloped El Halcón; the devil meant deliberate, snake-blooded murder, no less. He would be justified in plugging the hellion without mercy.

But he was a peace officer and had to give him a chance to surrender. His hands dropped toward his gun. And the utterly unpredictable happened.

The blue jay, skimming and wheeling through the brush, let go an outraged screech, as much as to say, "What, another one!" and darted straight for Slade's face.

Of course he zoomed upward the instant before reaching it, but Slade couldn't help dodging and flinging up his hand to ward off the attack. And the upflung hand struck a cluster of low-hanging dead branches that crackled sharply.

The dry-gulcher whirled, rifle swinging around. Slade drew and shot, left and right, a split second before the other pulled trigger. The rifle muzzle bucked up. The slug tore through the crown of Slade's hat. The dry-gulcher fell forward on his face without a sound, the Ranger's two bullets laced through his heart.

Slade instantly slid back into the denser growth,

his eyes probing the terrain, cocked guns ready for instant action. But nothing moved. No sound broke the stillness save the infuriated yells of the jay, which had shot upward like a popgun ball at the boom of the reports. Evidently the dead man did not have a companion.

Reassured by the lack of movement and the continued silence, Slade stepped forward. He glanced back the way he had come as a terrific crashing sounded, swiftly drawing nearer. He waited. A moment later Val Parker burst into view, both he and his horse bleeding from thorn scratches.

"Blast it! I couldn't stay back there with you maybe being killed!" he shouted, reining his mount back on its haunches.

"Guess that was asking a bit too much," Slade conceded. "Well, there's your dry-gulcher. *He* won't try it again."

Parker swore with amazing fluency and unforked.

"So you got him, eh?" he exulted.

"Yep," Slade replied. "Was close, though. Oh, shut up!" he called to the scolding jay. "Chances are you saved our bacon for us, but just the same you came darn near getting me my come-uppance."

"And if it weren't for you and your absolutely uncanny ability to figure things correctly, that sidewinder would very likely have gotten one or both of us," Parker declared. "How the devil do you do it?"

"I've had some experience with this sort of thing," Slade answered. "Those who ride the border of outlaw land learn not to miss much, if they hope to stay alive."

Parker shot him a peculiar look. "And that remark," he said slowly, "strikes me as being in the nature of a *double-entendre*." Slade noted that he pronounced it correctly.

"And," Parker added, apparently regarding his companion in a new light, "I'm beginning to wonder a little about something. Yes, I'm beginning to wonder."

"Okay, just so you don't wonder out loud," Slade said, with a smile.

"I won't," Parker promised; but the glance he bent on El Halcón was one of heightened respect.

10

"Well, let's look this punctured gent over a bit," Slade suggested. "Might uncover something interesting."

Squatting down, he turned the dead dry-gulcher over on his back, revealing a swarthy, pock-marked countenance, a slabbing, reptilian mouth, a broken nose and glazed, muddy eyes. He was of average height and build, with an expression of viciousness not even death could eradicate.

Parker's heavy black brows drew together. "Walt," he said, "I'm sure I've seen this hellion before. Just where or when I can't recall, but I'm sure I have."

"Any remembrance as to who he was with or talking to?" Slade asked.

Parker slowly shook his head, still staring at the evil dead face.

"No," he replied, "but it sort of comes to me that he was with or talking to someone I know. Who? I'm hanged if I know. Maybe I'll pin it down later."

Slade began turning out the dead man's pockets, revealing considerable money, a knife, and sundry trinkets of no significance. One article, however, he deftly palmed before Parker got a look at it. Something he wished to think on a bit before discussing with Parker or anybody else.

"Well, that takes care of that," he said, replacing the contents, save the one exception, of the pockets. "He must have had a horse, and it should be around somewhere close. Let's have a look. Just a minute, though, I want to glance over his hardware.

"Regulation iron and common to the section," he pronounced the fellow's rifle and the Colt forty-five in his holster. "Let's go."

A brief search discovered the horse, a good-looking bay, tethered to a branch. Slade glanced at the brand.

"Mexican skillet-of-snakes burn," he announced. "Can be interpreted whatever you wish. Easy, cayuse, I'll make you more comfortable."

He deftly stripped off the rig and piled it near the corpse.

"Suppose the sheriff should be told about this?" Parker said hesitantly. Slade nodded.

"Yes, he should know." He glanced at the sun. "It's still early, so I guess we'd better return to town and report what happened. He can pack in the carcass and put it on exhibition. Perhaps somebody will recognize it. We'll leave everything just as is for Chester to look over."

As they neared the town, Parker, who did not lack canniness, made a suggestion: "How about getting in touch with Judge Bowles first? He seems to think mighty well of you."

"A good notion," Slade agreed. "We'll take him along when we visit the sheriff."

"I'm afraid Chester has a sort of poor opinion of me," Parker remarked, with a chuckle. "And I've a notion he looks sort of sideways at you because of the El Halcón talk. So a little backing won't hurt."

"Tom will cool him down," Slade smiled reply. "If he needs help, we'll have Doc McChesney turn his wolf loose on him. When Doc really gets going there's usually a scattering."

"Judge" Bowles listened with profane interest to Slade's recital of the happenings on the ridge crest. He gazed at the young rancher and shook his head.

"Parker," he said, "you've been a good deal of a hell raiser and a headache to the rest of us ever since you landed in this section, but you've finally succeeded in getting yourself into company that will keep you stepping."

Parker's boyish grin flashed out. "Guess you're right, Judge," he conceded. "But, blast it! I like it!"

Bowles shook his somewhat grizzled head again and sighed. "You young hellions are all alike nowadays," he declared. "Now, when I was young—"

"You continually had the whole neighborhood

by the ears, you and your jokes!" Slade finished for him. "Oh, I've listened to what old-timers have to say about you. When it comes to giving advice to callow youth as represented by Val and myself, it would become you to tighten the *látigo* on your jaw."

Bowles grinned and did not argue the point.

"Let's go see Chet," he suggested. "Will he snort!"

Sheriff Chester started to do some snorting, all right, but Slade was in no mood for tantrums and quickly set the sheriff back on his heels.

"There's the evidence on that ridge crest for you to look over," he told Chester. "That's as far as your responsibility goes. You're not a judge and you're not a jury. If you find indications of an unlawful act you can have a warrant issued and put somebody under arrest. Until you arrive at that decision we can do without superfluous comment."

His eyes never left the peace officer's face as he spoke and that cold gaze added to the words had a chilling effect on the irascible Chester.

"Okay, okay," he grumbled. "I'll ride down there pronto. Just a waste of time. Nobody can ever get anything on you."

Slade looked at him, and suddenly the little devils of laughter, always in their clear depths, leaped to the front and confronted Chester with their gay warmth. The old lawman glowered,

93

then grinned, a rather sheepish grin but still a grin.

"Okay," he repeated. "You could talk a rattle-snake out of fanging, so what's the use of arguing with you. I don't mean to be unreasonable, it's just that I'm sort of beside myself of late, with things like this continually happening."

"And who can blame you," Slade said, his eyes abruptly all kindness. "Well, let's hope that things work out soon. And I've a notion they will."

"Somehow I got the notion, too," the sheriff admitted. "All right, boys," he said to his two deputies present, "grab that spare horse to pack the carcass and let's go."

When, after a bit, they reached the ridge crest, Sheriff Chester glared at the dead dry-gulcher.

"Snake-blooded hyderphobia skunk!" he growled. "A good chore, Slade, a raunchin' good chore. Wish I'd been along to help you do it."

Slade nodded. "Come here and I'll show you something else," he said. He led the way to the fringe of growth through which the trail was plainly visible and pointed to a stout tree branch that stretched out from a trunk at about breast high on a man of average height, and parallel to the distant trail.

"Look close," he said, and pointed to an abrasion on the upper surface of the branch. "See where the bark is scuffed and beginning to brown? That's where he rested his rifle when he took the shot at Val yesterday."

The sheriff peered with narrowed eyes. "Yes, I can see it, now that you point it out," he conceded. "But how you managed to spot it is more than I can understand."

He gazed toward the trail and shook his head. "A long shot, a mighty long shot."

"Not too long for a competent rifleman, as the hellion undoubtedly was," Slade said. "I'll show you."

He strode to where Shadow stood, secured his Winchester and returned.

"See that tree on the other side of the trail, the one with the whitish trunk? Now watch the east side of that trunk."

He slung the long gun to his shoulder as he spoke, ignoring the rest the tree branch provided. The muzzle instantly spurted smoke. The intent watchers saw a chip fly from the east side of the trunk.

Val Parker whistled. The sheriff and the deputies stared.

"Guess you made your point," conceded Chester. "Well, we'll pack this horned toad to town and put him on ice for folks to look over."

"And Walt and I will resume our interrupted journey to my domicile," said Parker. "We'll be in for the inquest tomorrow, if the judge plans to hold one, which I suppose he will."

"Of course he will," grunted the sheriff. "Will give him a chance to do something he considers funny."

After they parted on the trail below, one of the deputies remarked to the sheriff, "Well, after that exhibition of rifle shooting, how'd you like to have *him* on the prod against you?"

"I don't know what he is or what he ain't, and no matter what folks say about him, there's one thing I know for sure," replied Chester.

"And what's that, Chet?"

"He's a man to ride the river with!"

The others nodded solemn agreement to the highest compliment the rangeland can pay.

11

Slade and Parker covered three more miles and the rancher announced they were now riding over his Bar Cross spread. Slade eyed the range with a cattleman's appreciation of the good grass, frequent groves and thickets that provided protection from sun and storms, and ample water. And when they began seeing cows he was also impressed; they were improved stock of the best.

"Yes, it's a good holding," Parker replied to his laudatory comment. "I'll be doing all right if that blasted Henry bunch or others like them would just leave me alone."

"Been losing cows?" Slade asked.

"Quite a few," Parker answered. "Not many at a time, a score here, thirty or forty there, but it keeps up steadily and I can't stand too much more."

Slade nodded his understanding. No owner could indefinitely put up with such a drain on his resources. It was worse than the occasional spectacular running off of a large herd.

"Any idea where they go?" he asked.

"As I figure it, there's only one way they can go," Parker replied. "My range is shaped something like a boot, with the toe curving around and butting up against the hills to the southwest. As I see it, that's the only way they can get them across to New Mexico and the mountains. They certainly don't go north. That way they'd have to pass across Allen Curtis's holding and would almost certainly be spotted, sooner or later. And of course they can't shove them due west. That way they'd have to pass the town and the well-traveled trails that lead to it. So they must run them south by west. But we've kept tabs on that section continually, especially what appears to be the only practical trail across that portion of the Cap Rock hills."

Slade nodded again, but he was not much impressed by the latter portion of this statement. Experience had taught him that often there were hidden trails through the hill country of which the cattlemen were ignorant—though they were known to the outlaws—old Indian tracks and the like, with which most of the Texas hill country was crisscrossed.

Quite likely that was the case here. While Parker's hands were keeping tabs on what they considered the only logical route by which the stolen cows could be shoved west to New Mexico, the rustlers were sliding them through somewhere to the north or south. The outlaws frequent the hill country which to them is sanctuary, while cowhands whenever possible avoid it, being reluctant to leave the level prairie, which is their preferred habitat.

He wondered about the holding to the south, the Lazy JL, which was the property according to Parker, of a dissolute young Englishman named Ragnal, who relied on his range boss to run the spread for him. Such conditions might make for carelessness on the part of the riders, a lack of interest and little attention paid to what went on. To ride across the Lazy JL might well be easy going for the wide-loopers, with little to fear in the way of detection. That, too, could be the answer.

"I'm still plumb flabbergasted over the way you figured from the antics of a blue jay where the hellion was holed up," Parker suddenly remarked.

Slade smiled. "The birds and the beasts will tell you much, if you'll only listen," he replied. "They speak a very plain language to those who have learned to understand it. And learning to understand it may mean the difference between living and dying. More than once some bird or little critter has saved me from disaster. In hostile country, the change of an owl's whistle to a querulous whine is significant. Just as is the sudden cessation of a coyote's yipping. A wild pig bursting unexpectedly from a patch of growth shouts that something, perhaps inimical, is nearby. The vulture breasting the upper winds and planing lower and lower says that death is not far off and may lead you to what's left of the quarry you've been following. A whisper of disturbed wings in the darkness warns that what you think you are stalking may well be stalking you. If that jigger the sheriff is packing to town had paid attention to the jay and moved from the vicinity of its nest, he might have escaped the fate that overtook him."

"And if you hadn't understood what the jay was trying to tell you, it might be us being packed to town," Parker observed grimly. "I've a notion I've learned some things today that may come in handy."

"Not unlikely," Slade conceded, smilingly. "Well, I guess that's your *casa* directly ahead, is it not?"

"Yep, that's my place," Parker replied. "Not bad, eh?"

"Very good, I'd say," Slade answered. "As is everything else I've noted so far."

The Bar Cross ranchhouse was big, and old, but in an excellent state of repair. Corresponding were the barn, the bunkhouse and other buildings. No matter what else he was or where he came from, Val Parker was undoubtedly an efficient cattleman.

As they pulled up in the yard, a wrangler came to take over the horses. He was introduced to Shadow and the big black followed him to the barn.

"Critters will be taken care of properly," said Parker. "Come on in."

The living room, large, airy, and bright, was comfortably furnished. The wall decorations were somewhat unusual for a Texas ranchhouse. There were pictures of dogs and horses and some excellent paintings. Among them Slade recognized a sensuous Fragonard, a dreamy Turner, and a rollicking Hals. The latter two flanked a drawing of a stately mansion done in the Tudor style, which caught the Ranger's attention as much as the paintings. He gazed for several moments, turned to find Parker regarding him, on his face a half-amused, half-cynical expression.

"You appreciate those things, eh?" he remarked. He jerked his thumb toward the drawing of the house: "Sort of different from this shack, eh? I was born there."

"I'm not in the least surprised to learn it," Slade replied. Parker nodded.

"Thought you'd caught on. Those eyes of yours miss nothing; they seem to look right inside a man and see what's there. I hope, in my case, what you discovered isn't too bad."

"Not at all," Slade smiled. "Quite the contrary, in fact."

"Thank you," said Parker. "I'm most glad to hear it. Of course you know what a remittance man is?" Slade nodded.

"Well, as you've already guessed," Parker continued, "I'm in the nature of a remittance man, differing from the general run of the breed in one respect—I have never accepted the remittances."

"I'm not at all surprised to hear that, either," Slade interpolated.

"Thank you again," said Parker. "I'd hoped you would understand. Yes, I'm the black sheep member of a very staid and respectable and rather highly placed English family."

"Why the black sheep?" Slade asked. Parker shrugged his heavy shoulders.

"A woman, cards, alcohol, and a quick temper," he replied. "A mixture that can be relied on sooner or later to promote a grand scandal. Worked beautifully in my case. Result, the regretful but firm suggestion that I might do better elsewhere. In other words, sent in exile because I was an embarrassment at home."

"I see," Slade nodded.

"So I betook myself elsewhere," Parker resumed. "Gravitated to the West and cattle country. Quite a few of us around here, as you know. More up in Wyoming, especially around Cheyenne. Most of them will never make any permanent contribution to the welfare of the country. They live on their monthly or quarterly remittances from England. Seldom do any real work and want to pick up a fortune without effort. Which just isn't done." He paused to roll and light a cigarette, and then continued.

"It may seem strange that so many of us have come to the West and gotten into the cattle business. We of the English landed gentry know horses and stock breeding—taught it from childhood. Here is much the same thing, on a vastly larger scale. Naturally the business appealed to me, but I didn't have the money to buy property. So I went to work as a cowhand. Already knew about all there was to know about horses, and becoming proficient in the other angles of the work was only a matter of time and experience. I drifted all through the West for ten years—Texas, Arizona, California, other states. Liked Texas best. Saved most of my wages. Pretty good at poker, which helped. Finally managed to corral enough *dinero* to buy this comparatively small holding. Some of the boys I got friendly with in Arizona and New Mexico and California agreed to ride for me. Some of my hands are Texans, of course. They all get along together despite differences of opinion where riding gear and so forth are concerned. Sort of a cosmopolitan outfit. My cook is an old Mexican I got chummy with over around El Paso.

"As I said, I drifted around, got lots of experience, learned all I could about the cow business, so when I managed to tie onto a spread of my own, I knew all the angles. I've been doing all right.

103

"So that's the story of the black sheep," he concluded, adding with a chuckle, "were one to put any credence in the El Halcón yarns, which I don't, our cases might conceivably be deemed somewhat similar. Oh, well, black sheep have their own land, and it isn't a bad land for—black sheep."

"Ever consider going home?" Slade asked. Parker grinned.

"Perhaps later, when my wool gets a bit whiter. That is, for a visit; I'd never go back there to live. This country has got me and I'll never leave it. Incidentally, I'm a naturalized American citizen. So I guess I'm rooted in Texas. I repeat, I've been doing all right since I settled here, and as I said while we were riding, if such hellions as the Henry bunch will just lay off me, I'll continue to do all right."

"I think they will, before long," Slade said quietly.

"I'm getting the same notion, of late," Parker nodded. "Well, I'm going out to the kitchen and tell the cook to rustle his hocks and prepare us a snack; the boys will be in and eat later. Take it easy; I'll bring in some coffee pronto."

Left alone, Slade leaned back comfortably in his chair and pondered what he had learned. He was not in the least surprised by Parker's confession, for he had quickly read the man aright. There was much English capital invested in the country, and it was but natural that young Britishers, banished from home for some reason or other, or imbued with the roving and pioneer spirit inherent in the Anglo-Saxon, should turn to cattle country. The western cattle baron in his mode of living more nearly approximated that of the wealthy English squire than any other class in the country. It was not at all strange that those open-air lovers of dogs and horses should feel the lure of the rangeland and see in it opportunity to redeem themselves or recoup lost fortunes. Mostly, however, they lacked the ingredients essential to success in the cow business as in any other—the capacity for hard work and meticulous attention to detail. They were usually good fellows, likable and picturesque excrescences in the plains country, who wanted to pick up a fortune without effort; but like the ghost towns of the West, soon to vanish from the scene. Some were more adaptable.

Val Parker was a good example of those last. He did not shun work and through years of practical experience had learned all he possibly could about the business before entering into it. He would, Slade believed, make a go of it.

An interesting and complex character, the Ranger thought, an engrossing study.

But so were Robin Hood and Captain Kidd.

12

Parker returned with the coffee. He regarded Slade critically for a moment.

"Yes, I think things are going to change for the better," he said, without preamble. "Juan, the cook, has been with me a long time and I have learned to respect his judgment of men and affairs. He said, '*Patrón*, now that El Halcón, the just, the compassionate, is here, all will be well.'"

"I must thank Juan for his good offices," Slade replied gravely.

He did so, a little later, when Juan called them to their snack—which was bountiful—in fluent Spanish to the old fellow's evident delight. He bowed his head reverently to El Halcón and departed smiling.

"I wonder," Parker remarked, "do you always take everybody in tow? Even Dolf Chester, who is not given to such an about-face, appears to have drastically altered his opinion relative to you."

"Not everybody, I fear," Slade smiled reply.

"*That* kind don't count," grunted Parker. "Let me fill your cup."

They had just finished eating and were enjoying a smoke when a young cowboy rode a lathered

106

horse into the yard. Parker met him at the door.

"What's up, Bob?" he asked.

"It's the boss, Ragnal," replied the puncher. "He's got the 'D.T.'s,' got 'em bad. Raving like a centipede with chilblains. Ben Holliday, the range boss, thought maybe you could do something with him. We've already sent for Doc McChesney. Been going on like this for three days."

"Why the devil didn't you come to me sooner!" Parker demanded irritably.

"Holliday figured he'd come out of it by himself," said the cowhand. "He always has—this ain't the first time—but I reckon he never had 'em this bad before."

Parker turned to Slade. "I'm afraid I'll have to ride down there," he said apologetically.

"I'll ride with you, if you don't mind," the Ranger replied.

"Be mighty glad to have you," said Parker. "Maybe you can handle *this* situation, too. Let's go!"

Swiftly they got the rigs on their horses, a fresh mount being provided for the Lazy JL cowhand.

"It's just about an hour's ride at the rate we're going," Parker said as they headed south at a fast pace. "We should get there by sundown. Blazes! what a day this has been! Lucky we started out real early or we wouldn't have been able to get it all in."

"Time is relative," Slade replied. "The hours either fly or crawl, in accordance with what you are doing or hope to do. Fleeting hours can be dragging minutes, or vice versa."

"Never heard it put just that way, but I guess it's so," Parker conceded.

It was not quite sunset when they reached the Lazy JL ranchhouse. The cowhands were assembled in a tense and apprehensive group outside the building, from which sounded the screams and curses of its whiskey-maddened occupant.

Ben Holliday, the range boss, elderly, competent-appearing but with a nervous mouth, was introduced to Slade.

"He's in there," he said, unnecessarily, "laying on a couch with a gun in his hand. Swears he'll shoot anybody that tries to come into the room. He means it. Been going like that since Tuesday. Hasn't eaten a thing for three days. If he isn't quieted down and some food gotten into him he's a goner. Been threatening to turn that gun on himself. Liable to do it, I'm scairt."

Slade could catch some disconnected sentences amid Ragnal's incoherent ravings—

"Damn him! damn him! damn him! He's got his talons in me! He's holding that club over my head! He's trampling me down in the mud! Damn him! I'll kill him! I'll—I'll—I'll—"

"Wonder whom he's talking about?" Slade said to Parker.

"I haven't the slightest idea," the rancher replied. "I never knew he had an enemy anywhere; he certainly never spoke of one to me."

Slade nodded, his eyes thoughtful.

"You should have come to me sooner, Holliday," Parker remarked. "Maybe I could have done something with him before he became so violent."

"I tried to get hold of Mr. Curtis—he's just about his closest friend, I reckon," said Holliday. "But he was off somewhere, so I sent for you."

"You did right there," Parker agreed. "But now we're here, what the devil are we going to do?"

"There is another door to that room, is there not?" Slade asked.

"Uh-huh, but he's got a chair braced under the knob," Holliday answered.

"And just how is that couch situated, facing the front door?" Slade continued.

"Yes, so that he's looking right toward the door. Come over here across from the side window and I'll show it to you," Holliday said.

Following the range boss, Slade paused opposite the window.

"You can see the back of the couch from here—" Holliday pointed—"it's toward the window. Sort of a high back, so you can't see him."

"And about six feet from the window," Slade observed musingly. "Well, I think I know how it can be managed. Stand aside, Holliday."

"What you figure to do?" asked the range boss, his mouth twitching.

"Stand aside," Slade repeated. With his eye he measured the distance to the open window. It was broad and high. Then he raced forward and leaped.

To the gasping watchers, it seemed the mighty bound of a mountain lion. He went through the window feet first, throwing his long body down with a sinuous movement. His feet landed squarely against the back of the couch. Over it went, the screeching Ragnal beneath. The gun boomed as Slade hurled the overturned couch aside, the slug whistling past his ear. Shrieking like a banshee, Ragnal swung the gun around to bear on the Ranger; but before he could pull trigger a second time Slade's steely fingers closed on his wrist. The second bullet thudded into the ceiling. Then Ragnal screamed with agony as El Halcón's awful grip ground his wrist bones together. The gun thudded to the floor. Slade whirled him over on his face and held him helpless.

Val Parker came pounding through the front door, halted, stared.

"My—my God! The chance you took!" he gasped.

"Get a tie rope and bind his arms to his sides," Slade said. "That will render him nearer comfortable than any other way. If he tries to kick, tether his ankles."

Parker rushed back outside and reappeared a moment later with the piggin' string, the others streaming in behind him. Two minutes more and Ragnal, foaming and cursing but helpless, was placed on the righted couch.

Slade gazed down at the madman's contorted face, which smoothed out for an instant as the deeply violet eyes met Slade's steady gray gaze.

It was a youthful face he saw, delicately featured, handsome, with disdainful lips, that nevertheless bespoke a pitiful weariness—a face that was marred by the indelible traces of fierce, ungoverned passions. Just for a moment it remained immobile, then contorted once more, the lips forming a bitter imprecation.

With a sigh, Slade turned and took stock of the room. It was tastefully furnished, bordering on the luxurious. Opposite the couch was a fine grand piano which excited Slade's interest. He spoke to Val Parker in low tones.

"I sure hope Doc gets here soon. Right now the poor devil is on the verge of a complete nervous breakdown." Again he gazed at the piano, a really magnificent instrument by a famous maker.

"Does he play?" he asked Parker.

"Yes, and rather well," the rancher replied.

"Sings some, too. He loves music and it seems to soothe him when he's nervous and depressed from trying to keep away from whiskey."

Slade suddenly had an inspiration as Ragnal's voice again rose to a scream. He moved to the piano, adjusted the stool, sat down and ran his slender fingers over the keys with a master's touch. He thought a moment, played a soft prelude, flung hack his black head and sang a pathetic ballad of England, a song that would appeal to any exile. And as the great golden, metallic baritone bass pealed and thundered, the room grew strangely silent, for Parker and the others stood speechless, and Ragnal's yammering had ceased.

Glancing over his shoulder, Slade saw that the young man's face had once more smoothed. His lips were slightly parted, his wide eyes staring upward, and from them trickled slow tears.

The music ended in a last exquisite note, a last nostalgic verse:

"Still stand the cliffs of Dover?
"Still fair the English rose?"

It seemed nobody dared to speak. Ragnal lay motionless for a moment, then moved restlessly. Slade turned back to the piano and sang a simple but lovely song of *Méjico* which had gushed from the heart of some unknown poet who knew the simple people of the land below the Rio Grande, their lowly pride, their earthy longings. He sang another, and another, and finally left off playing when Val Parker touched his shoulder.

"Look!" Parker said hoarsely. "Look! He's asleep!" He turned to face the others.

"Gentlemen," he said, his voice quivering with emotion, "whoever says the day of miracles is past tells a damned lie!"

13

Doc McChesney, when he arrived a little later, Slade having meanwhile carefully cut the sleeper's bonds, had a rather more prosaic explanation which did not change Parker's mind.

"The basic cause of delirium tremens, resulting from excessive and protracted use of alcohol, is inflamed brain cells and frayed nerves," said Doc. "Rhythm of any kind is soothing, musical rhythm extremely so. A voice like Walt's would soothe an angry Gila Monster's nerves. Okay, I'll go to work on him. Keep some hot soup ready and we'll give him a feed when he rouses up. He'll be okay in a few days, until he gets to swiggin' again. Meanwhile, he can thank Walt for being alive. Wouldn't have lasted much longer even if he didn't put a bullet through his head, which he very likely would have done.

"Now he will probably sleep for hours—the longer the better—and when he awakens there's a good chance he'll be fairly rational; I don't expect any more violence from him. I'll stay here tonight, Holliday, but I want somebody to sit with him, and awaken me at once if he shows signs of coming out of it. Be sure and have that soup all ready to heat. If things work out as I expect them to, he'll be ready to eat. I guess that's all for now."

"And, Walt, I reckon we might as well head back for my place," said Parker. "What a day! And what a passel of chores you've managed to pack into it. Let's go. See you tomorrow, Holliday."

"Okay," said the range boss. "I'll set up with Ragnal myself, but I'll be around when you make it here."

As they rode home under the stars, Parker chattered animatedly about the day's happenings. Slade, on the other hand, was silent and preoccupied.

Finally Parker said, "Why so quiet, Walt? What's on your mind?"

"I'm still wondering just who Ragnal was talking about when he was raving and mouthing threats," Slade replied. "In my opinion, somebody is doing him a terrible injustice, or at least so Ragnal thinks."

Parker shook his head. "As I said before, I haven't the least notion who it could be," he replied. "Just the same I wish he could get out of here and go home where he belongs. His brother is dead and he is heir to the title and the Ragnal estates, which are large. He just doesn't belong in this country, and if he stays here he's going to go plumb to hell."

"Perhaps," Slade conceded, "but there is such

115

a thing as fighting temptation and overcoming it. I gather that you yourself could be cited as an example."

"I guess in a way you're right there," Parker agreed. "Only," he added, "I never resorted to alcohol as a vehicle of escape from my difficulties."

"Like fire, it can be a good servant but a very bad master," Slade nodded. "However, the physical and psychological make-up of the individual must be considered. To Ragnal it is plain poison. Well, we'll see."

"And I have a strange feeling," said Parker, "that you are going to save something more precious than Ragnal's life as you did today—his manhood. And I'm recalling something else old Juan, my cook, said: 'El Halcón! As did Our Lord in the days of old—he goes about doing good!' "

The following morning, Slade and Parker headed for Signal to attend the inquest. As they passed the brush-grown ridge where the dry-gulchers had holed up, Parker eyed the bristle of chaparral apprehensively. Slade shook his head.

"Nobody up there this morning," he said. "Birds are going about their business peacefully, and I've spotted a couple of rodents fooling around. Also, with the sun shining on the growth the way it is, I don't think anybody could move without attracting my notice."

"I wish I had your eyes," sighed Parker.

"My experience might be nearer the truth," Slade said, with a smile. "I hope you'll never need it."

"Might come in darned handy," Parker grunted. Slade chuckled and let it go at that.

Upon arriving in town, they cared for their horses and repaired to the coroner's office, where the body of the dry-gulcher was laid out for inspection. Parker again gazed long and earnestly at the dead face, the black bar of his brows wrinkling.

"I *know* I've seen this hellion somewhere," he reiterated. "I know it!"

"That's more than anybody else will admit," growled Tom Bowles. "The Henry bunch has got folks buffaloed. There's talk going around, Parker, that they took a shot at you because you've been sounding off about them."

"And I'll keep on sounding off," rumbled Parker, the hot glitter birthing in his dark eyes. "I'm not scared of the blankety-blank-blanks! And with Walt here on the job, it's *them* that had better be scared."

"You've got something there, feller," Bowles admitted.

The inquest was short, the verdict a foregone conclusion. Bowles was in no mood for jokes and rushed things through. The jurymen shook hands with Slade and congratulated him on a good chore. After which everybody thronged to the Hogwaller for a snort and something to eat.

Wingless Angel came over, sat down and began counting on his fingers.

"Yep, four," he concluded. "At this rate the Henry bunch is gonna end up short of skunks before long. Oh, by the way, I forgot those two bunches that gunned each other in the alley.

"Maybe one or two got their come-uppance there," he added hopefully. "Anyhow, they're getting thinned out."

"Yes, but Henry himself, whoever he is, is still mavericking around, according to all accounts," Slade remarked. "And that sort of a head can grow another body mighty fast."

"Uh-huh," said Wingless, who pulled no punches. "He's got everybody guessing, even though we have had a few suspects. To tell the truth, I sorta figured he might be Val, here. He sorta answers the description of Henry as handed out by folks who claim to have seen him. I shoved Val aside in a hurry, though. He's too blasted lazy for the chore."

"And I'd figure *you* might be Tarp Henry if you wasn't so busy all the time robbing folks right here," retorted the aggrieved Parker. "Why go out and work for your stealings when you can just squat here and have them brought to you."

Wingless chuckled and motioned the waiter to bring a drink.

"All joking aside," he continued seriously, "Walt has made more headway against the scoundrels in the short time he's been here than anyone else has been able to do since they showed up in the section. Come election time, if he's still sticking around, he gets my vote for sheriff. I understand Chester has had enough and doesn't intend to run again."

"Mine, too," declared Parker. Tom Bowles grinned.

"What do you say, Walt?" he bantered, his eyes twinkling.

"I fear it would tie me down too much," Slade smiled reply.

"Uh-huh, but it's time you settled down," insisted Wingless. "You're young, but you'll be surprised how the years will creep up on you. I know."

"He'll never be a spavined old coot like you," Parker remarked.

"Nor a bloated lard tub like some folks I could mention," Wingless returned.

Having mutually affronted each other they chuckled and set to on their food.

After they had finished eating, Parker offered a suggestion, "What say, Walt, suppose we ride over and see how Ragnal is making out? Plenty of time before dark."

"A good notion," Slade agreed. "Let's go."

On their way to the Lazy JL they met Doc McChesney returning to town.

"He's okay," said Doc, apropos of the patient. "Young, strong constitution. Will stay all right till he starts hitting the bottle again. One more bout like this one is liable to be his last. See you in town, Walt."

When they reached the ranchhouse, they found Ragnal pale, weak, and nervous, but rational. He held out a trembling hand to El Halcón.

"Mr. Slade," he said, "Holliday told me about what you did for me yesterday. Words are poor things with which to express gratitude, but if ever I can do you a favor, no matter what, please don't hesitate to ask it."

"You can do me a really great favor right now, Mr. Ragnal." Slade replied as he pressed the other's hand.

"Name it!" Ragnal instantly said. "It's yours before you ask. What is it, please?"

"Mr. Ragnal," the Ranger answered slowly, his steady gaze fixed on the young fellow's face, "just this—stop drinking."

Ragnal stared at him. "You mean it?" he asked thickly.

"I do," Slade replied. "That's the favor I ask of you, the biggest one you can grant. To you, alcohol is a poison. Your physical make-up is such that you can't take it. And, unfortunately, you are one who cannot taper off. There is only one way for you to stop, and that is to *stop*. Never touch it again from this minute on. You'll suffer, that I grant, but it's the only way, and it'll pay off big in the end."

Ragnal drew a long and quivering breath. "After what you did for me, there is nothing I can refuse you," he said. "I'll do it. I'll never touch another drop. I've been bad, foolish, stupid, but I don't think I'm a physical weakling, and when I give my word I keep it. I'll go through hell for a while, that I know, but I'll take it. You have my word."

Slade pressed the hand he held—hard.

"And right now a little coffee wouldn't go bad," Ragnal said, with a feeble grin. Holliday hurried to the kitchen.

They had finished, the coffee and were smoking when a horseman rode up to the ranchhouse, dismounted, and stood framed in the doorway. It was Allen Curtis, the Forked S owner.

"Come in, Mr. Curtis," said Holliday. Ragnal did not speak but lay gazing at Curtis.

Allen Curtis walked in, his step assured, graceful. He nodded to Slade and Parker.

"How are you, Ronald?" he asked of Ragnal. "I heard you were a bit under the weather. Figured a drink might do you good, so I brought along a bottle of my private stock." He produced it as he spoke and placed it on the table.

121

"Holliday, some glasses please," he ordered, rather than requested. Slade spoke.

"No," he said. "Mr. Ragnal is not drinking any more."

Curtis shifted his gaze and appeared to see him for the first time.

"Mr. Slade," he said, "I think you presume."

"It may appear presumption to you, Mr. Curtis, but to me it is a plain statement of fact," the Ranger replied.

Curtis continued to gaze, an inscrutable look in his blue eyes.

"I think," he said coldly, "that Mr. Ragnal should make his own decisions."

"Mr. Ragnal is in no condition right now to make decisions, so I am making this one for him," Slade answered. "Do—you—understand!"

The last words shot at Curtis like rifle bullets. He seemed to recoil, almost physically, from the Ranger's voice. Then his face darkened with fury. His left hand rose, thumb and first finger touching the left lapel of his coat. Slade smiled thinly.

"Don't try it, Mr. Curtis," he said. "If you do, you'll die."

For a moment their glances locked like rapier blades. Then Curtis's eyes slid away. He turned to Ragnal.

"I'm sorry to see you in such company, Ronald," he said. "This man is a notorious outlaw."

Val Parker rose to his full six feet and more of bulky height. "Curtis!" he roared. "Another crack like that from you and I'll take you by the seat of your pants and throw you out of here. And when I've finished with you outside, I'll throw what's left clean to the Forked S!"

Slade spoke, for the mad glitter was again blazing in Parker's eyes.

"Easy, Val," he said. "I think Mr. Curtis will prefer to depart under his own power."

Without haste, Curtis turned his back on them and strolled out, walking neither fast nor slow, and down the steps to his waiting horse. Slade sauntered after him to the edge of the veranda and stood watching him ride away.

Inside the room, Ragnal spoke, his eyes wide, his voice little more than a whisper: "He dared to stand up to him!"

"Ron," Parker replied, "if Walt Slade thought he was in the right and *He* was wrong, he'd dare to stand up to the Big Boss of the Range up above, and Allen Curtis is a long ways from being God!"

14

Slade returned to the room, sat down and rolled a cigarette, as if nothing unusual had happened. Ragnal regarded him curiously.

"Mr. Slade," he said, "did you mean it when you warned Curtis he would die if he attempted to draw that revolver he wears in a holster under his arm?"

"I meant exactly what I said," Slade replied. "I figured he is too fast to take chances with. The shoulder draw is a very fast draw if perfected, and I think Mr. Curtis is a man who perfects anything to which he sets his hand."

"He is the quickest man with a gun I ever saw," Ragnal observed.

Val Parker chuckled. "Know what they call *him?*" he said, gesturing to Slade. "The fastest gunhand in the whole Southwest. And the singingest man in the whole Southwest, to which you will doubtless agree if you recall anything of last night."

"I recall it vaguely," Ragnal replied. "Mr. Slade, would you please sing again?"

With a nod, Slade crossed to the piano and sang again the English ballad he had sung the night before. Ragnal lay staring at the ceiling, but this time there were no tears in the violet eyes, only a look of grim determination.

"Thank you," he said, when Slade returned to his chair. "You have a wonderful voice, and you are an outstanding pianist. Rather unusual accomplishments, are they not, for a cowhand?"

"Perhaps—for a cowhand," Slade acknowledged. Ragnal suddenly chuckled weakly and gestured to the table.

"When I first saw that bottle I wanted a drink," he confessed. "Now I don't."

"An ill wind that don't blow nobody no good," Val Parker misquoted cheerfully as he scooped up and pocketed the bottle.

As they headed for the Bar Cross ranchhouse, Parker remarked: "Well, I guess that takes care of Allen Curtis, so far as Ragnal is concerned."

"I'm not so sure," Slade differed. "There is something strange about the relationship between those two. Ragnal is afraid of him, and Ragnal is not a physical coward. I think it was Curtis he was raving about in his delirium. Yes, very strange. By the way, do you happen to know where Curtis came from?"

"Sabine River country I believe he claims," Parker replied. "Don't know anything about him prior to that."

Slade nodded thoughtfully and for some time was silent.

"Val," he said abruptly, "I'm going to head back to town; I want to send a telegram without delay."

"Okay, see you tomorrow, I hope," Parker replied, asking no questions, doubtless figuring they would not be answered, in which surmise he was correct.

The telegram Slade sent, addressed to Captain Jim McNelty, Ranger Post Headquarters, was short; but its contents caused the operator to stare.

When the message had clicked over the wires, Slade let his gaze rest on the operator's face.

"I understand," he said, "that the rules of your company forbid the divulgence of the contents of any message sent from this office. I would consider it a personal favor if in this instance the rule is strictly observed."

"Don't worry, it will be," the operator replied, and meant it.

"I would consider it a favor if you'll forget all about sending it," Slade added.

"I've already forgotten," the operator grinned.

"May be two or three days before you receive an answer," Slade told him. "Please hold it for me."

"I will, sir," the operator promised.

"Thank you," Slade said, and left the office. Outside he muttered to himself: "Now, *Señor* Curtis, I think we'll get a line on your origins, and, perhaps, just what your hold is on young Ragnal."

Twilight was falling and the nightly bustle of Signal was getting under way. Sauntering to Tom Bowles's feed store, Slade found him closing up shop.

"Well, how's the young lord?" he asked.

"Coming along nicely," replied Slade.

Bowles shook his head. "Pathetic," he said, "like so many of those young fellers who drift out here, slipping down the ladder rung by rung."

"He has been," Slade conceded; "but I've a notion he's going to start climbing back up very soon."

"Do you really think so?" Bowles asked dubiously.

"I do," Slade answered. "I have faith in him."

"Well, then, I guess he'll make it," Bowles said. "The way you handled that situation has got the whole town talking. A couple of Lazy JL hands were here this afternoon and they sure spread the story around. They said they wouldn't have given a busted *peso* for your chances when you dived through that window."

"There was really very little to it," Slade deprecated the feat. "Once he was on the floor with the couch on top of him it was easy."

"Oh, sure!" snorted Bowles. "Easy to tussle with a maniac with a loaded gun in his hand!

Your notion of what is easy, and mine, are slightly different."

Slade smiled, and changed the subject.

"Let's go eat," he suggested. "Been quite a while since breakfast."

"Soon as I lock the door," agreed Bowles. "Doc said he'd be there."

When they reached the Hogwaller, they found McChesney at a table fortified with a full glass. Wingless Angel sauntered over to serve them.

"Well, what now?" he asked Slade. "Feller, have you kept things hoppin' since you coiled your twine here! You've got everybody singing your praises."

"The spectacular that is sometimes wished onto one is always productive of morbid interest," Slade replied. Wingless chuckled.

"Nobody wished you through that window, so far as I've been able to ascertain," he differed. "That was precisely your own notion."

"Always taking up for some useless terrapin-brain," Doc McChesney snorted. Slade smiled and did not argue the point.

"Your friend Allen Curtis was in a little while ago," observed Wingless. " 'Peared to be in a bad temper, which is unusual for him. Was real snappy. Came in with a couple of fellers I don't recall seeing before, salty-looking jiggers but quiet and well behaved. They sat at that corner table over by the dance floor, talking and drinking for about half an hour, and then moseyed out. Maybe Curtis figured to sign them on, looked to be cowhands."

Slade nodded, and looked thoughtful. He was becoming quite interested in the doings of the Forked S owner. He was convinced that Curtis had some sort of a hold on young Ragnal and was using it to further some end of his own. What the hold was, and the end, Slade had not the slightest notion, and he had to admit that his interest in the affair was based largely on curiosity.

Which was all very well. But he was not at all satisfied with the progress he had been making. He had been sent to the Signal country not to save wastrels from themselves or ferret out the details of what appeared to be a private feud of some sort, but to run down an outlaw bunch that had been terrorizing the section. True, he had succeeded in eliminating a few undesirable characters who could well have been members of the outfit, but as to how said outfit operated, he still had only a hazy notion, and not the slightest idea as to who was its head. Well, perhaps things would work out; they usually did, often in a most unexpected fashion. And sometimes what appeared to be a disconnected thread worked into the pattern and proved to be the master strand by way of which the whole web could be unravelled.

Slade retired early, and once again the late hours of darkness found him riding into the western hills. When the first glow of sunrise ringed the hill crests with saffron flame he was well on his way to pay Uncle Ben Grady a visit. He believed that Uncle Ben and his mystery mine might well be the lure that would bring the Tarp Henry band into the radius of his loop.

Arriving at the old cabin in the clearing, he found Uncle Ben busy panning the sand bar.

"Just about cleaned her," said the prospector, after warmly greeting Slade. "Hard rain night before last and yesterday morning that trickle coming down there was swollen and yellow. Knew I had a good day ahead of me and got busy right away. Was good, one of the best. What you been doing with yourself? Come on in and have a snack and tell me about it."

Nothing loath, Slade accompanied him to the cabin, where a little later he enjoyed a good breakfast. Later, over coffee and cigarettes, he regaled Uncle Ben with an account of his adventures.

"You sure raise hell and shove a chunk under a corner," said Grady, shaking his grizzled head. "Everything peaceful here, no sign of Henry's hellions. Nobody else been around. Well, suppose we go out and look things over."

"Be glad to," replied Slade, who was still very curious about the unusual formations of the spot.

They repaired to the sand bank, where Grady displayed the results of his day's panning.

"Not bad, eh?" he remarked complacently.

"Very good, I'd say," Slade replied. "But if you can just locate the source of this pay dirt, what you have here will be peanuts. Blast it! there must be a way to get to where this comes from."

"Maybe, but I sure ain't been able to find it," said Grady. "Sometimes I doubt that anybody ever did."

"Whoever built the cabin and put those leg irons to use did," Slade declared. "Well, I'm going to give things a careful once-over."

He gazed up the mountainside. In the sunlight, the black cliffs seemed to reflect back a mocking gleam.

"Whoever built the cabin had a good reason for desiring a fairly permanent residence, one that would be comfortable and could be defended from possible attack," he remarked musingly. "It may have been Captain de Gavilan, or it may have been some other Spaniard who opened up a mine. Somebody took a lot of metal from somewhere around here, and the answer rests in that confounded upended chunk of rock."

For a long time he wandered along the creek bank, studying the opposing cliffs, estimating heights and distances, and was forced to admit that to all appearances they appeared unclimbable. After a while Uncle Ben called him in for a snack. Then he smoked a couple of cigarettes and sat pondering the problem, trying to put himself in the place of the prospector of former years who had hit on the treasure trove, of which the gold that Uncle Ben panned from the sand bank was but a meager gleaning.

In fact, Slade was reasoning by the method he used to out-think the outlaws, his uncanny ability to put himself in the outlaw's place and reason what he would do under similar circumstances. It was the real secret of Walt Slade's unusual success as a Texas Ranger.

Finally he went out and resumed his study of the terrain. Abruptly he got his inspiration.

He had paused to rest a moment in the shade of a tall tree that grew close to where the creek dived into the gorge, and he was admiring the sunset that was flaming in glory over the western hills. Leaning against the trunk, he idly traced the rough bark with his fingers. Suddenly a peculiarity in the bark formation attracted his notice. He turned to examine it.

Clear around the stout trunk was an indenture perhaps two inches in width. It was as if, many years before, the bark had been ground away almost to the wood fibre beneath—almost, but not quite enough to kill the tree.

"Now what in blazes did that?" he wondered to Shadow, who cropped grass nearby. "Looks almost like a rope had been tied around here and chafed the bark a lot over a long period."

His black brows drew together in perplexity, until the concentration furrow was deep between them, a sure sign that El Halcón was doing some hard thinking. He continued to trace the furrow abstractedly with his slender fingers.

Abruptly, his eyes glowed. He stared at the shallow furrow in the trunk, turned and gazed along the course of the stream.

"Shadow," he said, "I believe I've got it. I think I know how somebody used to get to the top of the hill. Not de Gavilan, I'd say—tree is hardly old enough for that; but it's plenty old, old enough for the later Spaniard prospectors to have put it to use. Yes, I'm sure I've got it figured out."

He hurried to the cabin, where Grady was preparing their supper.

"Uncle Ben," he said, "I've a notion I've got the lowdown on the problem. I'm pretty sure I've discovered a way to get to the top of the hill, the method used by whoever built this cabin and who opened up a mine from which they took a great deal of gold. No, not Sublett—goes back before his time, although it's just possible that he might have gotten gold here. Nor de Gavilan, in my opinion. How? I'll show you rather than tell you. Tomorrow we're heading for town with the mules. Quite a few articles we'll need."

Although evidently burning up with curiosity,

Uncle Ben rigidly refrained from asking questions.

They headed for town at daybreak, packing with them the gold Uncle Ben had panned from the sand bank. Arriving in Signal shortly after noon, Grady first deposited his gold at the bank, Slade accompanying him. Then they paused at the Hogwaller for a bite to eat.

After they had finished their meal, Slade drew a slip of paper from his pocket and handed it to Uncle Ben.

"You can take care of it while I have a talk with Tom Bowles," he said. "There isn't so much. Put everything in the stable with the horse and the mules and we'll pack it later."

Uncle Ben ran his eye over the list. "A new ax," he remarked. "The old one's plenty good to chop stove wood. And all them big nails. Figure to build another house? Or maybe you plan to chop your way up the cliff with the ax."

"Something like that," Slade smiled. "I'll tell you everything now, if you wish me to. I wanted to keep it as a surprise when I show you what I have in mind."

"Let her keep," replied Uncle Ben. "I just hope I don't bust wide open trying to figure it out. Okay, I'll get busy. Meet you here later."

And in sending Uncle Ben to make the purchases alone, El Halcón made a mistake for which he would pay bitterly.

• • •

When Uncle Ben entered the general store, two not too prepossessing individuals sauntered in behind him and pretended to bargain for some small articles at an adjoining counter. Meanwhile they noted with interest what the prospector bought. One was tall, burly, with alert dark eyes. His companion was small, wizened and fox-faced, and walked with a limp. After making a couple of insignificant purchases they strolled out shortly after Uncle Ben had departed with his truck.

"Now, what in blazes does the old hellion want with two hundred feet of rope?" the tall man demanded of his companion. "Anse, I figure there's something in the wind the boss should know about. We better get in touch with him right away. El Halcón rode in with the old coot, and I betcha he rides back out with him."

The other swore viciously. "That's the one I want to line sights with," he said, his voice a shrill whine. "I want to even up for this leg he gave me; I'll always limp."

"You'd better lay off him or you'll end up getting what Zeke and Withrow got when they tried to brace him in the saloon, per the boss's orders. And what Penrose got up on the ridge. That big devil is poison."

"I've a notion to slide along behind him when

he rides out of town and get a chance to put a slug through him," whined Anse.

The other shot him a look of contempt. "Why don't you use your head for something else 'sides holding up your hat?" he said. "We've got a chance to tie onto enough to put us all on easy street and you'd figure to spoil it just to even up for a hole in your blasted leg! What do mining fellers want with rope by the hundred-foot? To go down a hole or a shaft with, of course. They've hit on the old mine sure as shootin'. You tangle this thing for Tarp and I sure wouldn't want to be in your boots. Hanker for a little taste of an ant hill or the spines of a cholla cactus? You know how Tarp works."

Anse blanched slightly, and his eyes shifted away from his companion's angry gaze.

"All right! all right!" he grumbled. "Have it your way. What we going to do?"

"We're riding to see the boss right away," said the other. "Come on."

15

After dinner in the Hogwaller, with everything cared for, Slade and Uncle Ben went to bed. They arose before daybreak, got the pack on the mule and headed west. Slade carefully watched the back trail as well as the terrain over which they passed, but he sighted nothing untoward. When they arrived at the cabin in the clearing, he at once got busy.

In addition to the ax and the rope, Uncle Ben had bought a good saw, a large augur and a couple of long and heavy bolts.

"What do you want with all that rope?" Uncle Ben wondered. "Figure to drop a loop on that blasted hilltop and climb up?"

"That's the general idea," Slade answered, with a grin. With the new ax he felled two stout trees and cut the trunks to eight-foot lengths, which he trundled to the water's edge near the old tree with the grooved bark and proceeded to spike the logs together securely until he had a rough but serviceable raft. Next he searched out a small tree with a perfectly round trunk. With the saw he cut a length of the trunk, bored holes in each end, and after spiking spreadled uprights to the raft, fitted in the bolts and had an efficient windlass to which he attached a handle.

"Get the notion?" he said to the still mystified

Uncle Ben. "I want to get a look at the other side of the bulge around which the creek curves, so I figured out a way to do it. And I'm pretty well convinced I'm not the first to figure it. See the mark on the tree trunk? That mark was made, a long time ago, by a rope tied around the trunk and chafing the bark. Somebody else went into that canyon by way of a raft anchored to this tree. Plumb easy. You just hop on the raft, pay out the rope till you get around the bulge and into the canyon. When you want to come back, you just haul yourself back with the rope. The chances are the folks who first conceived the experiment drew themselves back by hand, with several pulling on the rope, but I've fitted the raft with a windlass so that one man can easily manipulate it. Understand, now?"

"Oh, well," said Uncle Ben resignedly, "I've eat a heap of fish in my day, so I reckon it's only fair for the fish to eat me. Which is just what will happen if that rope happens to bust."

"That sisal can take it," Slade replied cheerfully. "But if you wish, I'll try it out first alone." He chuckled at Uncle Ben's indignant glare.

"That's enough for today," he said, glancing at the rose and gold of the sunset sky. "Now we'll cook something to eat and take it easy, and get an early start tomorrow. Bet you a hatful of *pesos* that before that sun goes down again, you'll be hauling gold out of your lost mine."

"That is if I ain't shoveling coal down below," sighed Uncle Ben. "But you seem to always know what you're about, so I'll take a chance."

They were at the water's edge soon after dawn the following morning. The raft was loaded with a couple of lanterns and several big candles in addition to the ax and a second coil of rope.

"Might have some climbing to do, and our way could lie through the dark," Slade explained.

One end of the rope was secured to the tree trunk, the other to the windlass, the slack neatly wound around the barrel. They shoved the raft into the water and Slade began slowly paying out the rope as the current caught the unwieldly craft. Old Ben stood with a long pole, ready to fend off from the cliffs or any rocks they might happen to encounter.

Almost instantly, near disaster struck them. Belatedly, Slade realized that he had gravely underestimated the force of the current. It seized the raft as in a giant hand and hurled it downstream. The windlass handle was whisked out of his grasp and spun around and around madly, the rope fairly smoking off the barrel. He gripped the humming twine and put forth all his great strength, and was nearly jerked into the water.

With a despairing yell, Uncle Ben dropped the pole and leaped to his assistance, but a moment later had to let go the rope, grab the pole and work with might and main to keep them from being dashed against the rocky face of the bulge.

By a terrific effort, Slade got the raft under control and they made it around the bulge, with the black rock flickering past their faces. The rope bounced against the cliff and that helped, reducing their run-away speed.

"That was close," Slade panted. "I was careless. Know better next time and it'll be easy. Just don't let the slack run out after the raft is in the water; that's where I slipped up. Next time everything will be okay."

"If there ever is a next time," groaned Uncle Ben. "We ain't out of this yet."

"Nothing more to worry about," Slade reassured him. "See, there's a place to land—a little strip of sand at the base of the cliff. Shove her over with the pole and we'll beach her."

Uncle Ben deftly manipulated the pole and a moment later the raft bumped and ground to a stop on the little beach, which was not more than a dozen yards in width and grown with a straggle of sotol and other brush.

The rope was not quite paid out, so they hauled the craft onto the beach and proceeded to give their surroundings a once-over.

"Well," Uncle Ben grunted disgustedly, " 'pears like we took a prime chance on a drowning for nothing. The cliffs are straighter here than farther back."

Slade nodded. It was undoubtedly true. "But

you'll notice there's a ledge running up the face of the cliff," he pointed out, "and it looks to be climbable."

"Uh-huh," Grady agreed without enthusiasm. "And you'll notice it stops a hundred feet or so up. And from there on to the top, the cliff is plumb sheer."

"No argument there," Slade conceded, "but I'm playing a hunch. We're going to climb that ledge. Perhaps we can see something from up there."

"Uh-huh, some more water," Uncle Ben predicted gloomily. "Let's go."

He followed Slade in the scramble up the ledge, which wasn't very steep. It widened as they progressed, and sloped inward like the petal of a flower. Soon they were following a sort of narrow lane walled by stone.

"Here's something interesting," Slade remarked. "Water trickling down here, and it certainly isn't dripping from the cliff top."

"Didn't I say we'd see more water," Uncle Ben reminded. "Don't mean much."

"It probably means considerably more than you think," Slade differed.

Soon they were nearing the crest of the ledge, which curved around the bulge of the cliff. Slade uttered an exclamation.

"Now take a look," he told Uncle Ben.

Directly ahead, a jagged opening split the face

of the cliff. They hurried forward, pausing, and peered into the gloomy hole.

"Well, Uncle Ben," Slade said, "looks like we've hit it. Look into the cave. See the steps cut in the rock?"

The old prospector's lined face was aglow with excitement. "Darned if it don't look like it," he admitted. "We going in there?"

"First we'll return to the raft and fetch along the rope and the ax and the lanterns and candles," Slade decided. "Looks like our way is going to run in the dark, all right. This is getting decidedly interesting."

It quickly became more so to Slade after they entered the cave, armed with the two lanterns and a supply of candles.

"Uncle Ben," he said, "somebody, a lot of somebodies, climbed these steps ages before the Spaniards came here looking for gold. The steps are worn and hollowed out by the pressure of untold numbers of feet."

"Sure looks that way," the prospector agreed.

As they climbed the worn stair, Slade paused frequently to examine the rock walls by the light of the lantern.

"Quartz," he said at length, "which is gold-bearing rock. As I mentioned to you before, the lava which faces the outer cliffs is in the nature of frosting on a cake. A peculiar and unusual formation, but it has parallels elsewhere in the world. This region was once highly volcanic, just like the Ashes Mountains country in the Guadalupe Range, but this is far older. Now the Cap Rock is not considered volcanic, but once upon a time, ages ago, it was. This is but a manifestation of Nature's eccentricities. Highly interesting."

Old Ben, on the other hand, was more interested in the roof of the tunnel, which glowered above their heads. It was seamed and broken, and from it fell slow drops of water.

"Golly! What a hole!" he muttered. "Look at the loose rocks up there. A touch would bring 'em down on our heads."

"Don't talk loud and don't stamp your feet," Slade cautioned. "Any undue vibration might start them falling. Unlikely, but not beyond the range of possibility; best not to take chances."

The bore twisted and turned, but always with the very steep ascending grade; had it not been for the steps hewn in the rock, its ascent would have been well-nigh impossible. As it was, the going was laborious but not difficult.

"Blown out by steam or a gas explosion untold millions of years ago, when the volcano was going strong," Slade observed.

They proceeded slowly and cautiously for perhaps half an hour. Then abruptly the stair ended and they found themselves in a broad and lofty cave, the darkness of which the lantern pierced for but a short distance.

"Good gosh!" Uncle Ben suddenly exclaimed, "what's that thing over there?"

As they approached the shadowy object, holding the lanterns high, it revealed itself to be a statue some ten feet in height, hewn and carved from the living rock of the mountain.

Scaled and feathered, bird-like and serpentine, its stony eyes stared fixedly at the darkness. The beaked countenance was serene, but the calm on it was dreadful. The calm of inhuman cruelty, the cruelty that many of the ancients attributed to beings potent for good, who could yet watch the sufferings of humanity, if not with rejoicing, at least without suffering themselves.

"Quetzalcoatl!" Slade exclaimed. "The Aztec god of the air, the sky lanes, the lightning and the storms. The most revered deity of the Aztec pantheon. Uncle Ben, this high temple was once a shrine of Quetzalcoatl. It is generally conceded that the Aztecs were in Texas before they invaded Mexico, conquered the Toltecs who resided there and took over the land, and along with it many of their customs and beliefs. Quetzalcoatl, in a way, corresponded to Hiawatha of the North American Indians. The Toltec legend says that he disappeared by way of the ocean, with the message that in a future age his brethren, white like himself, would come from the ocean, land and rule the country, a legend which proved serviceable to Cortes and his Spaniards when

144

they arrived in what is present day Mexico. At first, the Aztecs, who had adopted the legend and believed in it, treated the invaders with courtesy and reverence. Didn't take them long to become disillusioned, however."

"Could be," Uncle Ben conceded, gazing dubiously at the statue, "but the darn thing gives me the creeps."

Slade chuckled, and moved closer. "Look here," he said.

Fronting the statue was a stone slab set on supports, about waist high, seven feet long by three wide. Its slightly concave surface was bored at intervals with small holes. The stone was discolored by dark stains.

"The altar upon which sacrifice was offered to the god," Slade explained. "Those holes were to drain off the blood."

Gazing at the ominous slab, he visioned the scene enacted there hundreds, perhaps thousands of years before—the sacrifice stretched on the slab, the priest robed in scarlet and with his headdress of the feathers of the Quetzal bird, his eyes burning with fanatical fire, the obsidian knife raised high. The downward flash of the knife, the scream of agony from the sacrificial victim, then the slow, soft splash of the flowing blood.

Perhaps Uncle Ben visioned something of the same, for he exclaimed, "Let's get the heck out of here; I don't like this place! Which way shall we go?"

"To the right," Slade replied with the plainsman's uncanny instinct for direction even underground and in the dark. "We should see light and hit the outside soon, I figure."

"I hope so," growled Uncle Ben. "I'm beginning to think I'm not cut out to be a miner; I don't like dark holes in the ground."

"Chances are placer mining is your dish," Slade replied. "That way you can always work in the sun. But if this thing turns out to be something in the nature of what we hope it will, the chances are you soon won't need to go in for any kind of mining."

They proceeded in the direction Slade indicated, carefully examining the floor of the cave for possible pitfalls or obstructions, and discovered none.

"That statue is highly interesting," Slade remarked thoughtfully as they trudged along. "Also, it explains something that has been puzzling me—how the Spaniards happened to discover the gold in such a seemingly inaccessible place. Hundreds, maybe thousands of years before, the Aztecs founded this temple to Quetzalcoatl. It was their habit to build their temples to the god of the air in lofty places. Perhaps the course of the creek was different in those days and the approach to the cave less difficult. The Aztecs also mined gold, which they used for ornaments and vessels. The legend of the mine came down through the years and the Spanish prospectors heard it from the Indians they contacted, and figured out the way to reach the hilltop."

"Sounds reasonable," admitted Uncle Ben. "Those old jiggers were smart, all right."

"Yes, they were," Slade said. "And with a keen nose for anything in the nature of treasure. I wouldn't be surprised if there are a number of hidden diggings in the hills that they concealed as best they could and kept quiet about when they had to pull out suddenly for some reason or another, usually an Indian uprising."

"I see light ahead," Uncle Ben suddenly exclaimed.

"Yes, we're about out," Slade replied.

It was light, a greenish glow that strengthened as they proceeded. Soon they saw it was the sun shining through a fringe of verdure. A moment more and they stepped out of the cave into a flood of brilliant sunlight and gazed about.

They were standing in a shallow cup perhaps a quarter of a mile in diameter and walled about by low cliffs.

"As I expected," said Slade. "It's a lesser crater of the old volcano that has weathered down in the course of the ages. Now filled with earth formed by the erosion of the lava cliffs for millions of years. Quite a bit of brush and some trees scattered around."

"And by gosh there's another old cabin!" Uncle Ben exclaimed, pointing to the remains of a log structure a hundred yards or so distant.

"Let's look it over," Slade suggested.

The roof of the cabin had long since fallen in, but the stout log walls still stood firm. The door sagged on rusted hinges. Scattered about were cooking utensils of tarnished copper, and rotting pieces of home-made furniture. And bolted to the walls were more leg irons.

"The mine is somewhere near, you can count on that," Slade observed. "More of the slaves who worked it were kept here, I've a notion. Evidently quite a going concern. I'd say this shack is about the same age as the one down in the clearing, which has been repaired and has a new roof. Well, let's see what else of interest we can find."

He turned to gaze toward the face of the nearby cliff. His gaze centered on what, flanked on either side by dense thicket, looked like the coping of a very large well, circular and built of rough stone blocks. Rising on either side were stone posts grooved at the top.

"There it is," he said. "There's the shaft to the mine. Those stone posts were to hold a windlass barrel, which has rotted away. Let's have a look."

They hurried to the shaft mouth, which was

about ten feet in diameter, and peered down into its thickening gloom.

"Not more than twenty feet to the ground below," Slade said. "This will be easy. Our rope is better than fifty feet long. We'll halve it, knot cross pieces between the two strands and have a rope ladder. Fasten that to a log we'll cut and lay across the shaft onto those posts and down we go."

16

The chore was soon accomplished. Slade made sure that everything was secure and descended to find himself in the beginning of a tunnel boring into the mountain.

"Send down the lanterns and then come along and we'll look things over," he told Grady. "Uncle Ben, I think you're all set to get rich," he added, as the prospector joined him at the bottom of the shaft.

"Son," said Uncle Ben, "why don't you stay here with me and help work it? Anyhow, half of it is yours. Fact is, I've a notion that under mining law you could claim the whole thing, by right of discovery."

Slade smilingly shook his head. "Thanks, old-timer," he said, "but I have other things to do. Everything that comes out is yours. I have a few *pesos* laid aside for a possibly rainy day, and a man in my line of work doesn't need much money."

Uncle Ben shook his head regretfully, but the tone of Slade's voice told him it was no use to argue.

"Shall we look her over?" he asked.

"Yes," Slade replied. "I'm curious as to just what we'll find. We have plenty of time before dark."

They relighted the lanterns, made sure they had plenty of candles if needed, and entered the tunnel, which had a downward slope.

"I hear water," Slade remarked, a little later.

"Good!" said Uncle Ben; "I'm thirsty."

A few minutes more and they came upon a little stream which flowed from beneath the rock wall on the left. The water was cool and sweet. Its course was down the tunnel after crossing it to wash the opposite wall.

"In my opinion this is the brook that comes out of the cliff and tumbles down to join the creek," Slade observed.

"The one that washes the gold out to the sand bank," said Uncle Ben.

"Presumably," Slade agreed.

A little later the tunnel widened greatly to the right. A few more steps and in the right wall yawned a dark opening higher and wider than the tunnel. Slade paused to examine the walls.

"Not natural," he said. "This is a drift gallery of a mine. Doubtless there are others. And look there." He pointed down the main tunnel.

All along the right bank of the stream were great heaps of gravel, tons of it.

Old Ben made a dive for the nearest and began pawing through it. After a few minutes' search, he drew forth a rough, round, dull-colored pellet and hefted it in his palm.

"What do you think of that?" he asked, passing

it to Slade, who likewise estimated the weight.

"Gold, all right," he said. "The same as you have been washing from the sand bar. Now let's have a look at this gallery, and any others that exist."

Others did exist. For a long time they toiled through dry and dusty tunnels, each of which was several hundred feet in length.

"Well," said Slade when they returned to the natural bore down which the stream flowed, "it's a mine, all right, but just about worked out. Nobody is going to take a million from it, but in my opinion there's enough metal in those gravel heaps to fix you comfortable for life."

"Sure looks that way," Uncle Ben exulted, "and it looks, too, like the fellers who dug all that out must have left in a hurry, for some reason or other, don't you think?"

"Yes," Slade agreed. "Perhaps they fled from an Indian uprising. Let's look about a bit more— down along the stream bank."

Closer inspection with the lanterns revealed not only more gravel heaps but also rude cradles not unlike the one Grady used to pan the sand bank. In that dry and sunless air, the wood had remained remarkably firm.

"They're workable," Slade decided. "All they need is a mite of grease. You're provided with all you need to set up shop here in the cave. Can do your washing here. You'll only have to pack down the metal, which you can haul up the shaft with the rope ladder. And the mystery of the gold in the sand bar down below is explained. During the working of the mine, a great deal of gravel must have fallen into the stream, considerable gold along with it. When the creek is high after a rain, the gold on the bed is disturbed and some of it washes down the fall to the sand bank. Also when the water is high, it quite likely dislodges some from the heaps and carries it along. Been doing that for many years. Well, let's get back down to the cabin; I'm hungry."

"Me, too," said Uncle Ben, "plumb starved."

When they shoved the raft into the water, Slade told Uncle Ben to man the windlass handle. He nodded with satisfaction as the husky old prospector drew the raft back upstream to the sand bar without difficulty.

"And when you come down the creek, just be sure there's no loose slack," he warned. "That's where I made a mistake and when the slack ran out we got a devil of a jerk. Keep the rope tight around the windlass barrel and pay it out slow and easy and you'll have no trouble."

The following morning, before he rode to town, Slade watched Uncle Ben manipulate the raft loaded with tools and supplies, which he did without difficulty. He was pleased to note that when the raft was beached around the bulge, the rope dropped beneath the surface of the water, so that only a look at the tree trunk from close range would reveal its existence. If anybody came snooping around while the prospector was at work, it was highly unlikely his whereabouts would be ascertained. Confident that the old fellow would make out all right and of the opinion that he was in no danger of being molested in the immediate future, Slade headed for Signal with a mind free from care, so far as Uncle Ben was concerned.

Upon arriving in town, and before he stabled his horse, he paused at the telegraph office.

"Here it is, sir," said the operator, passing him a sealed envelope. "Came through this morning, early."

Slade tore open the envelope and read Captain Jim's answer to his request to learn everything possible about the Ragnal family and Allen Curtis. It ran:

Lord Ragnal. Baron of Realm. Head of highly respected English family dating back to the Norman conquest. Quite wealthy. One son Ronald. Heir to title and estates. Conduct not too good. Embarrassed family. Sent packing. Presumably somewhere in America.

Allen Curtis. First cousin to Lord Ragnal. Not wealthy. Breeder of horses and cattle in England. Came to America three years ago. Dealt cards on Sabine river boats. And in Sabine country saloons. Owned half interest in small ranch in Newton County. Sold out to partner. Dropped out of sight. Will try and learn more.

A satisfied expression in his eyes, Slade folded and pocketed the message.

"Thank you," he said to the operator.

"For what?" that worthy asked blankly. "I don't remember doing anything for you, sir. Thought you just dropped in to pass the time of day."

"Hombre, you're okay," Slade chuckled at the other's discretion. The operator looked pleased.

"Shadow, it's sure interesting how things work out," he remarked as he led the big black to his stall in the stable. "We try and do a favor for a couple of folks and all of a sudden the mystery is, I believe, solved, and the problem perhaps on the way to a satisfactory solution. Strange, isn't it?"

Aside from a dubious snort, Shadow refrained from comment.

After caring for the horse, Slade headed for the Hogwaller and something to eat. He found Val Parker there, talking with Wingless and Tom Bowles.

"Where you been?" the rancher asked. "Thought maybe you'd trailed your twine."

"Nope, just dropped over for a visit with Uncle Ben," Slade replied.

"How is the old coot?" Parker asked.

"Fine as frog hair," Slade said. "Busy panning away. He'll make out." He asked a question of his own, "How's young Ragnal making out?"

"He's fine, too," answered Parker. "Up and around and's beginning to look great. Says he has a hankering for a drink every now and then but takes a good swig of coffee instead and forgets all about it. Wouldn't have believed such a thing were possible, but there it is."

"His physical make-up is not that of one whose system demands alcohol," Slade explained. "He drank to forget, and as a relief for mental strain. With the incentive gone or lessened, the craving will leave him. In periods of depression, it may return, to an extent, but I don't think he'll ever succumb to it again. I'll drop over and see him tomorrow or the next day."

"A good notion," said Parker. "Your presence will have a good effect on him and strengthen his resolve. After all, it was to you he made his promise never to drink again."

"And he'll keep it," Slade answered.

"Bad for business, but I'm in favor of it," sighed Wingless. "And after all I got enough copper-lined gents around to keep me going. Besides, they say alcohol mostly affects the brain, so jiggers like Tom and Val don't have to worry no more than a terrapin."

"Guess you're right," retorted Bowles. "If

156

we had any brains we'd never come into this rumhole."

Feeling a bit weary after a strenuous week, Slade took it easy the rest of the day and went to bed early. Mid-afternoon of the following day, however, found him arriving at the Lazy JL ranchhouse.

"How's your boss?" he asked of Ben Holliday, who helped him put up his horse.

"He's feeling low," Holliday replied. "Don't know what's the matter with him. Allen Curtis was here this morning. Don't know what Curtis had to say, but it sure upset him. Glad you've showed—I expect you'll be able to perk him up a bit."

"Yes," Slade answered, "I think I will."

When he entered the ranchhouse, Ragnal was sitting in a chair, staring moodily out the window. His eyes brightened when Slade appeared.

"I'm sure glad to see you, Mr. Slade," he said. "Very, very glad. Take a load off your feet." He called to the cook to bring coffee and cake.

Slade sat down in an opposite chair and rolled a cigarette, his gaze resting on the other's face. He touched a match to the brain tablet and said, "Ragnal, just what is Allen Curtis holding over you?"

17

The rancher looked decidedly startled. Then he drew a deep breath.

"I guess I might as well tell you," he replied. "I can't see as it will do any harm, and you seem to be able to straighten anything out. I killed a man over in east Texas, at least Curtis says I did."

"That so?" Slade did not appear much impressed. "How'd it happen?"

"Curtis and I came across together," Ragnal explained. "As perhaps you already know—you seem to know everything—he is my cousin. We knew some fellows from England who had settled over this way, so we came to Texas. Curtis is rather handy with cards and he went to work dealing on the Sabine river boats and in a couple of saloons over there. I stuck with him for a while. One night there was a fearful row during a poker game in a saloon. I was blind drunk and remember very little about it, although I guess I started it. I remember nothing of what happened during the next twelve hours or so."

He paused, and shuddered, as if overcome by some dreadful memory.

"The next morning," he continued, "the dealer I accused of cheating and who hit me and

158

knocked me out, was found dead in the mouth of an alley, a knife in his back. There was quite a to-do over it, but nobody seemed to have any idea as to who did it. Then Curtis took me aside and told me that I killed the dealer, and that he saw me do it. Naturally I was panic-stricken or near to it. Then Curtis said that to save the family disgrace, he'd never tell if I'd promise to never return to England. I promised, didn't see what else I could do. After which I came over here and with money I'd saved from my remittances, I bought this little spread, cheap, from a fellow who was sick of the country and wanted to go home, where he would be welcome, seeing as he'd never done anything wrong, just having been a sort of wanderer. I thought maybe I'd do all right here in a new country. Perhaps I would have, but Curtis followed me here and bought the Stanton place up to the north of Val Parker's holding."

Ragnal paused again and with nervous fingers tried to roll a cigarette. Slade deftly manufactured one and passed it to him.

"Thanks," he said gratefully, and then resumed; "Very soon he began asking me for money. I gave him all I had. Then I went in debt to the law firm in New York that handles my father's American interests. They were pleasant to me, figuring no doubt that eventually I'd inherit the estates. But there was a limit as to how deep they'd go. The only thing I have left is this little ranch. This morning Curtis demanded that I sign it over to him."

"As the price of silence," Slade interpolated.

"That's right," Ragnal replied. "So you see what I'm up against."

"And Curtis encouraged you to drink, I suppose?" Slade observed. Ragnal nodded.

Slade regarded him fixedly for a moment. Then: "Ragnal," he said, "didn't it ever occur to you that by doing what he did, Curtis made himself an accessory after the fact, to employ a legal term, one who aids or shelters an offender with the intent to defeat justice? If he brought a charge against you, he would also bring one against himself and be facing a penitentiary sentence. And with such a sordid set of circumstances involved, it would be a stiff one."

"Why—why I never thought of it," Ragnal replied.

"But I'll wager Curtis has," Slade said grimly, adding "and with only his word to back up the charge against you, the chances of you being convicted of the killing, even if it came to trial, which it never would, are absolutely nil. You have nothing to fear from Curtis so far as legal action is concerned, an action he would not dare bring."

Ragnal's eyes were exultant. "I just knew you'd find a way to straighten things out!" he

160

exclaimed. "What shall I do, confront him and tell him to go to hell?"

Slade shook his head, "No, not yet," he answered. "For there is another angle to consider. If you were to die, or never return to England and be disinherited, Curtis would inherit the title and the estate, would he not?"

"Why, yes, I suppose he would," Ragnal admitted. "He's next in line."

"So now you see the motive back of this skulduggery," Slade said.

"But what shall I do?" Ragnal asked helplessly. "I'm all confused."

"Play along," Slade said. "Act just as you always have, except where the drinking is concerned. Stall. Try and make him believe you are going to sign the spread over to him, but need a little time to think on it and figure what to do. Even if you did sign, it would mean nothing. Don't under any circumstances let him realize that you have caught on. Otherwise your life may well be in serious danger. He is a ruthless killer, and shrewd. Play along, and *leave Allen Curtis to me.*"

A long time afterward, when he was confiding in Val Parker, Ragnal remarked, "I don't think I'm exactly a physical coward, but when he said that, the look in his eyes scared the devil out of me; it was terrible! I never saw anything like it, made me feel all crawly inside."

The cook arrived with the coffee and cake,

bowed reverently to El Halcón and looked very pleased at his Spanish greeting. A little later, Ragnal asked an indirect question, "I wonder if by any chance it was Curtis who stuck a knife in that poor dealer's back?"

"It was," Slade replied, unequivocally. Ragnal shuddered.

"He's a devil," he muttered.

"He's a prime specimen, all right," Slade agreed. "The sort you run up against only about once in a lifetime, fortunately. Absolutely snake-blooded, as the saying goes. Which is really an injustice to the snake, who never bothers anybody so long as he is left alone, and fights back only in self-defense."

After the coffee and cake were dispatched properly, Ragnal remarked, "Really, I believe I feel up to a ride. What do you say, will you look things over with me?"

"Be glad to," Slade replied. "Let's go."

They got the rigs on their horses, Ragnal expressing his admiration for Shadow with a true horse lover's enthusiasm, and set out in the red-gold glow of the late sunshine.

It was fine range, Slade decided, a continuation of Val Parker's pastures, and even better watered. The cows grazing on the lush grass were good stock. He complimented Ragnal on their excellence.

"Holliday is a good man, loyal and efficient,

and the boys are good hands," Ragnal apportioned the credit where it was due. "Holliday's only weakness is that he hates to make decisions, but when I assure him that anything he does will have my sanction, he goes ahead."

Slade had already read that characteristic in the range boss's nervous mouth.

"Yes, the sort that needs a reassuring hand, otherwise okay," he replied.

"I intend to learn all there is to learn about this business," Ragnal declared. "I'm beginning to take an interest in it."

Slade smiled slightly but did not comment. They rode for some time in silence.

"It *is* a beautiful country," Ragnal suddenly observed, gazing to where the hills leaped up against the sky, ringed about with sapphire and amethyst, and the emerald billows of the western peaks catching the level light. "Yes, the kind of a country where a man feels he can stretch out. Harassed and worried as I was, I really didn't notice it, but with my mind free from care, I can appreciate it."

Slade glanced sideways at his companion and his lips quirked. The leaven was working, as it had on many another who looked with seeing eyes on this land of wild grandeur, its desolation redeemed by its promise unbreakable of ultimate rich reward to those who dared brave its rugged austerity.

They rode home under the stars. Ragnal's eyes were those of one who looks to new and pleasing vistas. Slade was pondering how to drop a loop on the wily Tarp Henry, who, it appeared, had everyone in the section nicely bamboozled. He chuckled to himself at the thought of the sensation when Henry's real identity would be proven.

However, he was quickly grave again. The problem was not yet solved, although he believed the plan he had formulated might work.

Slade spent the night at the Lazy JL. The following morning, after breakfast, he headed for Val Parker's *casa*.

"Careful, and watch your step," was his last word of warning to Ragnal. "Don't change your attitude toward him by one iota. Act just as you always have. String him along and make him believe you are going to accede to his wishes. I think you're smart enough to do it, but no slips. Make one and very likely your life will be forfeit. I've a notion he's getting a bit worried over the way things have been working out; they haven't been too good for him of late. I won't be back here for several days; the canny devil might get suspicious. Not beyond him to figure things out correctly if he is given a hint of what's in the wind. I'll be seeing you."

18

When Slade arrived at the Bar Cross ranchhouse, he found Parker in a very bad temper.

"I lost another batch of stock last night," the rancher explained. "Near to fifty head of prime stuff. The hellions ran them off my north pasture, less than three miles from the house. The nerve of those sidewinders! I expect 'em to snake out the kitchen stove next!"

"Even red hot," Slade smiled. "Your north pasture, and close to see the *casa*, you said? Suppose we ride over there for a look-see."

"Okay, if you want to, but I figure it just a waste of time," grumbled Parker. "I was over there—was aiming to run those cows in here, and some more, for a shipping herd. I looked the ground over and there was no tracking them. That grass springs right back up after it's been trod on and doesn't leave a trace of anything that's passed over it. Just like what I've been told about the Staked Plains up to the north."

"Perhaps," Slade conceded, "but we'll see. Sometimes horses do leave traces that can be followed. Get the rig on your cayuse and let's go."

When they reached the place, near a waterhole, where Parker said the beefs had been in the habit of spending the night, Slade dismounted and carefully quartered the ground around the spot. For nearly fifteen minutes he wandered about, bending over from time to time to study the grass. Finally he walked a straight line and nodded his head with satisfaction.

"Here is it," he called to his interested watcher. "Here is the trail the wide-loopers left. Val, your cows went north."

"But that's ridiculous," Parker protested. "To do that they'd have to pass across Curtis's land, and he keeps a close watch on things up there; they'd be taking a big chance of being spotted."

"Well, he didn't keep a close enough one last night," Slade replied dryly. "They went north, veering a bit to the west."

"How do you know?" Parker asked incredulously.

"Come here and I'll show you," Slade invited.

Parker unforked and joined the Ranger. "Bend down," Slade told him. "Bend down and look close to where I'm pointing. As you said, the grass quickly springs erect after being trodden down, especially when the sun strikes it. Okay, but notice this grass head. You'll see it's partly broken, the head dangling against the stem. And the break is fresh, has hardly begun to brown."

With his face almost against the ground, Parker peered to where El Halcón indicated.

"Yes, I can see it, now that you point it out,"

he said slowly. "But otherwise I'd never have noticed it. What kind of eyes have you got, anyhow?"

"It's just that I knew what to look for," Slade replied. "Now come along and you'll see another and another cut stem, leading always north by west. A horse's iron not only treads down the grass, if it is worn and the edge rather sharp, it also quite frequently cuts the stem. Even a new shoe will sometimes do it. One of the horses ridden by the rustlers has a worn shoe and makes an easy track to follow. Understand?"

"I guess so," sighed Parker. "Is there anything you don't know?"

"Plenty," Slade smiled. "But experience teaches, if one is not altogether stupid and careless."

"What are we going to do, trail the blankety-blanks?" Parker asked.

Slade gazed northward for a moment, then shook his head. "No, not just the two of us," he answered. "I've a notion there are six or eight in the bunch, possibly more. We're returning to the *casa* and pick up three or four of your hands, if they will come. Then we'll see what we can do, that is if you don't mind the chance of getting mixed up in a corpse and cartridge session."

"I won't mind," Parker replied grimly. "The boys won't either; they're itchin' for a go at those hellions. Come on!"

Less than an hour later, Slade, Parker and four of the Bar Cross hands left the *casa*. All were armed with sixgun and rifle, and the hands were as eager as their boss to come to grips with the outlaws.

"If it is the Henry bunch, maybe we can clean up the whole kit and caboodle of them," observed Parker.

"It's the Henry bunch, all right, or a portion of them," Slade stated definitely.

To his followers' surprise, he did not head north by west to the waterhole, but followed the Signal trail, which ran due west.

"If somebody happens to be keeping tabs on the *casa*, this will throw them off," he explained. "I can pick up the trail of the cows when I need it."

"What I can't understand," said Parker, "if they headed west up to the north, how the devil did they get through the hills. I understand there's not a trail up there that cows can travel."

"Sometimes there is a trail which is not known to the general public," was Slade's noncommittal reply. "We'll see."

Not until the brush-clad hills were looming close did Slade turn north. He slowed Shadow's pace and rode close to the fringe of growth that sprawled out on the prairie, his gaze fixed on the bristle of chaparral.

They covered nearly three miles of slow going.

His companions watched him mostly in silence and wearing an air of expectancy. Abruptly he reined in and sat gazing at a stand of tall growth that, so far as the others could see, was exactly the same as what they had been passing. They looked bewildered when he said, "There it is."

"I'll be darned if I see anything that looks like a trail," said Val Parker. "Walt, you sure?"

"I am," Slade said, swinging out of the saddle and walking slowly along the edge of the growth, his glance fixed on the ground.

"If I wasn't, this would certainly make me so," he remarked, pointing to the grass at his feet. "More broken stems, a lot of them. The cows were shoved here not many hours ago. Now take a close look at the brush. Notice how right here the leaves are browning, some of them beginning to shrivel. It's an old trick, but it works. I've run up against it before. I'll show you."

He walked to the growth, stooped down and grasped one of the slender trunks. A tug, and it came out of the ground, easily, revealing an end sharpened as a stake. He tossed the bush aside, removed another.

"See how it's done?" he said, as a chorus of exclamations spiced with vivid profanity arose. "The brush that hides the trail grows out on the pasture in the course of the years. The fact that a trail existed is forgotten, even if there was anybody around to notice it when it was visible.

The hills are crisscrossed by such tracks, mostly made by Indians traveling south to Mexico on raiding forays, and back. Look way up the slope, near the hill crest where the growth is sparse, you will notice what looks like an indenture in the brush, if you look close and know what you're looking for. Somebody figured there was a trail up the slopes, did a little investigating and found there really was, and decided to put it to use. They cleared a narrow passage through the brush, then replaced the cut bushes and small trees by sharpening the ends of the trunks and driving them back into the ground. Got a mite careless, though, a bit too sure of themselves, and neglected to replace the cut brush with fresh when the leaves began to turn and wither, which takes quite a while with this sort of vegetation. All right, turn to and help clear out this loose stuff."

Everybody went to work with a will, plucking the cut brush from the ground and throwing it aside.

"By gosh, he's right!" exclaimed Val Parker, peering ahead. "There's a trail going up the sag, wide enough for two men to ride abreast. Looks sort of like a shallow ditch."

"Beaten down by myriads of moccasined feet and, later, the unshod hoofs of Indian mustangs," Slade explained. "The ground is beaten so hard that rain water runs right off it and nothing will grow on the surface of the trail. Down here on the prairie, grass has covered the trail and the brush has hidden it. Make a careful search and quite likely you'll run across some more of a similar nature."

"And the blasted Henry bunch found out about it and used it to run off cows!" sputtered Parker.

"That's about right," Slade conceded. "Would also provide a good get-away bolt hole if they should happen to need it. Well, here we go!"

Mounting, they rode up the narrow trail. The thick vegetation met overhead, interlacing into a natural pergola, through which flowed a golden twilight varied by splashes of brilliant sunshine edged with amber and ruddy bronze. All was peaceful and no sound broke the cathedral hush, but El Halcón knew that death waited at the end of the trail.

As they rode, he explained his plan. "In my opinion they'll lay over for the night somewhere in the zone of broken country below the hills, which is called the breaks. They'd hardly risk running the cows west over the more open country during the daylight hours. Besides, those heavy beasts will be in no shape to tackle the plains without a night and day of rest. Once on the prairie, they'll push them fast and they'll want the cows in a condition to take it. I figure we can hit them after they make camp. Then the advantage will be ours. We've got to be careful, though; it's a shrewd and salty bunch, and the gent who calls himself Tarp Henry has brains."

"Any idea who he is, Walt?" Parker asked.

"I have a very good notion," Slade replied. "However, I prefer not to talk about him just yet; there's a bare possibility that I could be mistaken, although I don't think I am. Either way, he'll keep, and he's still to run down, which may prove considerable of a chore. All right, now, take it easy; it still wants several hours of sunset and I don't want to leave the hills until near dusk. They may be keeping a watch on the back trail, although I rather doubt it. But in a game like this, make a mistake and it's very likely to be your last."

At a leisurely pace they continued up the old trail. After a while the crest was reached, but the trail flowed on, winding down the opposite sags, always with a westerly by slightly south trend.

"I'd say it runs straight to the New Mexico mountains," Slade observed.

"Sure looks that way," Parker agreed. "Wonder why?"

"There were times when the migrating bison did not put in an appearance on the plains to the east, and there was plenty of good game in the mountains. Deer, bear, javelina pigs. And the Indians didn't hesitate at a wolf steak if nothing else was available. Primitive man, like his prototypes of today, followed the trail to food. Plenty followed this old track."

"And are still following it, in a way," Parker observed.

"Exactly," Slade conceded. "Predatory beasts always frequent the hills and prey on the inhabitants of the lowlands."

Dusk was already falling and Slade did not hesitate to continue down toward the breaks, which were wild and rugged. However, he slowed the pace a bit and grew even more vigilant.

"Use your ears, and use your noses," he told his companions. "If you catch a whiff of wood smoke or hear a cow bleat, let me know at once."

Val Parker chuckled. "Swell chance we've got of hearing or seeing or smelling anything before you do," he said.

"Never can tell," Slade answered. "Somebody in our bunch may have an extra keen nose. Ease up a bit more."

It was growing very shadowy under the interlacing growth, although the brush was thinning a trifle. Slade rode warily. He did not think the outlaws would have a sentry posted on the trail at some distance from their camping spot, but it was not impossible and he was taking no chances.

Overhead, seen through the rifts, the scarlet and gold of the sky was fading, the edges of the few small patches of cloud taking on a steel-gray tint. Birds in the thickets were singing their sleepy songs, their dulcet notes but serving to accentuate the soft hush that shrouded the wastelands. Sounds would carry a long way and Slade expected ample warning before they drew too near the outlaws' camp; if his surmise was correct, they would bed down the herd for the night and the coming day here in the lonely fastness of the breaks.

The sky deepened from gray to purple-black, through which a star peeped inquiringly. Slade slowed his posse still more against the chance of a hoof kicking a stone and sending it clattering. He instinctively felt that they were closing in on the quarry.

Abruptly he uttered a low exclamation.

"They're there! No great distance ahead. Smell it?"

His companions sniffed sharply. "Believe I do smell smoke," whispered Parker. "Listen! What was that?"

"A steer grumbled," Slade replied. "Hold it, we're closer than I thought; air's moving a little and holding the smoke back. Quiet, now, perhaps we can hear something else."

They did, a moment later, so loud and clear as to seem startlingly close, the cheerful whinny of a horse.

"Watch your bronc!" Slade snapped. "Be ready to grab his nose if he starts to answer."

The cowboys leaned forward as one man, hands

ready. However, the well-trained cow ponies made no attempt to reply. Slade glanced about. In the fast fading dregs of light he saw that the growth to their left was a bit thinner.

"In there," he whispered, Shadow setting the example. "Come on, a little farther. Here this'll do."

They had reached a little cleared spot where grass grew sparsely. Slade dismounted, as did the others.

"Will they stand and keep quiet?" he asked Parker, apropos of the horses.

"Yes, they're trained to and are dependable," the rancher replied. "We chose 'em carefully when we set out. Don't have to worry about your cayuse, of course."

"Not in the least," Slade stated definitely. "He'll stay right here till I call him, and you could pass within a yard of him in the dark and not know he is here. All right, now, we slide down the trail on foot till we sight their camp. Careful, and don't make the slightest noise. If they catch on and are ready for us, we'll get a reception we won't like. I've got to give them a chance to surrender, but I doubt if they'll take it. If they don't, shoot, and shoot straight and fast."

The others grunted their understanding. Slade only hoped their aim would be as good as their intentions. He knew that, contrary to popular opinion, cowhands are usually not very good shots, especially in the heat of a desperate battle. All he could do was hope for the best. Parker, he knew, was handy with a gun, so perhaps the odds against them would not be too heavy.

As they slipped silently down the trail, Slade experienced a disquieting feeling, a feeling that he had carelessly overlooked a small detail that could turn out to be darned big.

"Blast it! I should have replaced that cut brush before we left the prairie and started up the sag," he told himself. "The chances are there'll be nobody around down there to notice it, but then again there might be."

The chance that some members of the outlaw outfit, perhaps the leader, whom Slade did not believe would be with the bunch assigned the routine chore of running the cows to New Mexico, would spot the cut brush and the open mouth of the trail and quickly deduce its meaning gave him a chill along his backbone. Even now the devils might be stealing along behind them, waiting to catch them in a deadly cross-fire. He strained his ears to catch any sound in the rear, but could hear nothing. Well, it was too late now, if he had made a slip, to do anything about it. He concentrated on what was ahead.

19

At a snail's pace the posse crept along, Slade in the van, Parker crowding close behind him. Now they could make out the sound of rough voices, and occasional bursts of laughter. The wide-loopers, suspecting nothing and elated over a good haul, were in high spirits. The posse glided on, rounded a bulge of brush and halted.

Directly ahead was a fairly large clearing, grass-grown and watered by a little stream that trickled from a spring. Over to one side they could just make out the dark clump that was grazing cattle. Close to the spring a fire burned, the flames leaping in the still air and casting a wide glow of light. Pottering about the fire, waiting for it to burn down to a bed of coals, was a man preparing to cook a meal. Five more lounged about, smoking and talking.

"Keep to the right where you can jump back into the brush if necessary," Slade whispered to his followers. "Let's go!"

With quick, easy steps he strode forward into the circle of firelight, a gun in each hand, the others close behind him and fanning to the right.

His voice rang out: "Elevate! You're covered!"

Caught utterly unprepared, the outlaws gaped and mouthed, glaring at the grim figures facing them with drawn guns. It looked like they would be taken without a shot fired.

Slade spoke again: "In the name of the State of—"

The words were wiped from his lips by a sound, the sound of horses' irons clashing down the trail.

The outlaws heard it, too, and knew what it meant as quickly as did El Halcón. They scattered in every direction, going for their guns. Instantly the peaceful night was a pandemonium of hideous uproar. The booming of the guns, the bellowing of the frightened cattle, the neighing of startled horses, yells, screams, curses rent the air.

Slade's foresight saved the posse from annihilation. With a single bound, Parker and the hands were in the brush, shooting as fast as they could pull trigger. Back and forth gushed the orange flashes, spurting through the clouds of smoke. Slade whirled to meet the onslaught from the rear.

Into the firelight stormed two horsemen, yelling and shooting as they came. Both Slade's guns let go with a rattling crash. One of the riders spun from the saddle as if struck by a mighty fist. The other slumped forward, caught his balance and fired pointblank at the Ranger. The slug grained the top of Slade's shoulder and hurled him sideways with the shock. Another bullet, coming across the fire, ripped the sleeve of his shirt. He fired left and right, and again. The wounded horseman flung up his hands and plunged headlong to the ground. Slade spun around toward the fire, guns ready. Suddenly he realized there was nothing to shoot at. Bodies were strewn on the ground, and that was all.

"Two got away!" bawled Parker, blood streaming down his face and dripping from his left hand. "There they go, around the herd!"

Slade bounded forward, Parker close behind him. But directly in front of them were the terrified cows, milling about, scattering, effectually blocking their way. Before they could disentangle themselves, Slade heard the beat of fast hoofs dimming away down the trail. Parker heard it, too.

"Come on," he yelled, wild with excitement. "Come on, we'll get the broncs and run 'em down." He whirled and started back toward the fire.

"Hold it!" Slade thundered. "They've got a head start. Besides, they know the lay of the land and we don't; we're liable to ride into another trap. One tonight is plenty. Sometime I think I'll trade brains with a terrapin and come out ahead in the deal. Let's see if anybody is badly hurt."

"A couple of the boys got it, I don't know how bad," panted Parker. "No, I ain't hurt—just scratched a couple of times. You all right?"

"Nothing to worry about," Slade replied as they headed back to the fire.

"Anyhow we did for six out of eight," exulted Parker. "Not a bad average, that."

Besides the dead outlaws, two of the Bar Cross hands were stretched on the ground, one bleeding profusely from a wickedly gashed upper arm, the other with a bullet through his thigh. Slade hurried to examine the wounds.

"Not too bad, but bad enough," he told Parker, who was swearing softly to himself and swabbing at the blood that still trickled from a scalp wound. He stood up and whistled a clear note. A moment later Shadow came pounding down the trail, snorting inquiringly.

From his saddle pouch Slade took salve and bandage. Soon he had the wounds padded and bound up, the bleeding reduced. The injured punchers puffed cigarettes and swore cheerfully.

"Cut myself worse shaving, many a time," declared the man with the bullet-torn arm.

"A little blood-letting now and then is good for a man," said the other, cherishing his punctured leg. "See you got hit in the head, where it didn't do any damage, Boss," he added to Parker, with the familiarity of long and close association. "Someplace else and you might have got hurt."

"If you think you're going to get paid while you're hobbling around pretending that mosquito bite keeps you from doing any work, you got another guess coming," Parker retorted.

"That's telling him, Boss!" chuckled his fellow sufferer. "But when did he *ever* do any work?"

One of the unwounded hands, an old-timer, was getting busy around the fire.

"Plenty of good chuck and coffee laid out all ready to fry and b'ile," he said. "While the rest of you fellers look things over, I'll throw together a surroundin'. I reckon we can all use it."

"Fine notion," Slade applauded. "Food and plenty of hot coffee will be good for the wounded men. Now, Val, I'll take a look at your head. See you got a nicked wrist, too. A little salve and plaster will take care of them."

The chore finished, Slade's next move was to examine the slain outlaws.

"Hard-case-looking hombres," commented Parker, who accompanied him.

"Yes, they are, and rather more intelligent-appearing than the usual brush-popping scum," Slade said. "Recognize any of them?"

Parker shook his head. Then he glanced about as if to make sure none of the others were within hearing distance.

"Walt, there's something I want to tell you," he said. "Maybe I should have before, but I wasn't quite sure in my own mind, although I became pretty well convinced later that I was right."

"How's that?" Slade asked, interested.

"Remember the horned toad you killed up on the ridge, the one who tried to dry-gulch us? And maybe you'll recall that I said at the time that the hellion had a familiar look, that it seemed to me that I'd seen him with somebody. Well, later it came to me all of a sudden where I'd seen him. I didn't mention it to you then, though I reckon I should have, because you knew that Allen Curtis and I didn't get along too well, and I didn't know how you might take it. That fellow worked for Curtis quite a while back. I'm sure of it."

"Why didn't some of Curtis's hands recognize him when he was put on exhibition?" Slade wondered.

"Because when he was with Curtis, none of the boys who work for Curtis now worked for him then. When he bought from old Branch Stanton he took over Stanton's riders. But they didn't seem to cotton to him and it wasn't long before all of them had quit and gone to work elsewhere. Guess that dry-gulcher quit then, too, so I reckon it doesn't mean much."

"May mean more than you think," Slade said quietly. "Now I have something to show *you*." He drew a gold coin from his pocket and handed it to Parker.

"Why, it's an English sovereign!" exclaimed the rancher. "Worth the same as the pound sterling, about five dollars. Where'd you get it?"

"From the pocket of that dry-gulcher," Slade

replied. "I didn't show it to you at the time for a somewhat similar reason as yours for not telling me he worked for Curtis. At that time I wasn't sure of anybody and had no notion of whom I might be looking for. Right then nobody was under suspicion, which meant everybody was. Understand?"

"Yes, I guess I do," Parker replied slowly. "Wonder where that devil got it?"

"Hard to tell," Slade answered. "May have been given to him, may have stolen it. Anyhow, it must have come from someone who has or had access to English money."

"That's sure for certain," Parker agreed. "Let's look these sidewinders over; maybe we can find some more."

They didn't, but they did unearth a surprisingly large sum in good United States currency.

"Hellions have been doing all right by themselves," Slade commented. "Divide it up among the boys; they've earned it, and I've a notion they can use it to better advantage than the county treasury, where it'll go if the sheriff gets his paws on it."

"You're darn right," chuckled Parker as he pocketed the *dinero*. Abruptly he turned and looked Slade straight in the eye.

"Walt," he said, "do you suspect something off-color about Allen Curtis?"

"Only that he's the gentleman who calls

himself Tarp Henry, after a notorious Oklahoma owlhoot of that name," Slade replied. Parker whistled.

"Wouldn't have suspected him of being that good," he said, "but after what he pulled in the Lazy JL ranchhouse that day, trying to get young Ragnal to drink what he knew darn well was plain poison to him, I never trusted the blankety-blank and figured him capable of any sort of skulduggery. Tarp Henry! Well, I'll be hanged!"

Feeling that Parker, who was a true friend to Ron Ragnal, had a right to know, Slade repeated what Ragnal told him about his dealings with Allen Curtis. Parker swore with wholehearted fervor, then looked pensive.

"And I suppose," he said, "it was really Curtis who stuck a knife in the poor dealer's back and then led Ragnal to believe he did it while blind drunk."

"That's my opinion," Slade conceded.

"Well," Parker elated, "we've darn near busted up the so-an-so's gang for him, I'd say. About ten altogether, I believe."

"Yes, but we still haven't a thing on Curtis that would stand up in court," Slade reminded him. "They say Tarp Henry seldom leaves any witnesses alive; we've been emulating him in that respect. If we'd grabbed one of the hellions we might have persuaded him to talk to save his own neck. Well, there appears to be nothing of significance in this bunch of junk; put it back in their pockets for Chester to look over."

"Do you figure Curtis's cowhands are part of his bunch?" Parker asked.

"Highly unlikely," Slade replied. "He'd be too smart for that. The chances are he makes sure they are all in town, on a bust with bonus money for good work, whenever he plans to pull something."

"They are in town a lot, especially at night," Parker observed.

"Quite likely the bunch has a hangout somewhere in the hills, where they get together to plan things," Slade added.

"And if you could locate that hangout?"

"A difficult chore," Slade answered. "I've thought of that, of course, but I'm saving a search for it as a sort of last resort." Parker nodded his understanding.

"Come and get it!" suddenly bawled the old cowhand who had taken over the chore of cooking.

"We'll take a look at the horses later," Slade said. "Brands might tell us something; unlikely, though. Let's eat."

It was a good meal and a jolly one, and the wounded men had a full share. The hands laughed and joked, but Slade was mostly silent.

"What you frowning about, Walt?" Parker

suddenly asked. "You look as if you want to bite somebody."

"I do. Myself," Slade answered morosely. "I can't get over the stupid blunder I made in not replacing that cut brush."

"Nobody can think of everything and everybody makes mistakes," Parker comforted. "The rest of us didn't think of it, either."

"Yes, but you haven't had the experience with the owl-hoot brand I have," Slade returned. "I should have thought of it, especially as once before I ran into three varmints coming up a trail I figured was clear. Only a timely stampede saved me from getting my come-uppance. I was shoving along a bunch of cows I'd recovered, and when the shooting started they went hogwild and stomped a couple of those gents flat."

"And what happened to the other one?" asked Parker.

"He died," Slade said shortly.

"Which for brevity and total explanation I think is hard to equal," Parker commented.

"Well, I guess we might as well spend the night here," he added. "Don't you think so? When the boys took the rigs off the horses those gents who rode 'em won't be needing again, they found blanket rolls. So with a good fire going we should be comfortable; and I've a notion Bob and Emory will feel more like riding in the morning than they do now. Right?"

"Yes," Slade agreed, "but we're posting sentries on the trail in both directions. I don't intend to get trapped again. Two-hour shifts for all able-bodied gents. First, though, let's have a look at those horses."

They did, with scant results. "I recognize two of the brands as from the Sabine River country," Slade remarked to Parker. "Can't say as to the others. May mean nothing, however, horses can be bought, traded, stolen, and show up a long ways from where they were foaled. It is a bit interesting, though, two of them from around the Sabine. Something in the nature of a tie-up."

"That's what I'd say," agreed Parker. "Any notion how you're going to drop a loop on the hellion?"

"Yes, I have, in a way," Slade returned. "I'm going to play a hunch, maybe it will work out; I believe, and hope, it will, and before somebody else dies, which will very likely be the case if he gets another bunch together. Which won't take long."

He did not elaborate on his plan, and Parker asked no questions.

20

Slade's precaution proved needless, for the night passed without incident. After breakfast the following morning, there being ample provisions remaining, preparations were at once made to head for Signal. The bodies of the slain wide-loopers were roped to the saddles of their horses, the recovered cattle rounded up and gotten under way. The two wounded hands insisted they were able to ride and proceeded to prove their contention. Slade felt easy about them, for superficial wounds meant little to such rugged young fellows.

It was a slow and tedious drag with the plodding cattle and the lead horses, and the afternoon was well along when they passed from the hills onto the open prairie. Here the band split up, the uninjured punchers rolling the cows on to their home pasture, the wounded hands, who were beginning to show the effects of the long ride, accompanying Slade and Parker to town. For the Ranger decided it best that Doc McChesney give them a once-over and keep them under observation for a couple of days in what he called his hospital.

Signal was used to sensations, but even seasoned old-timers stopped and stared as the grim cavalcade clattered along the main street to the sheriff's office.

Sheriff Chester met them at the door. He also stared. "For the love of Pete!" he bawled. "What you been doing—robbing a cemetery?"

Parker told him, vividly and in detail. The sheriff outdid all previous attempts at swearing.

"Well, I'd say that just about cripples the Henry bunch, if those hellions were a part of the outfit," he concluded. "I doubt if we'll have to worry about them any more."

Slade did not agree but refrained from saying so.

The bodies were unloaded and laid out for inspection, the two wounded hands delivered to Doc McChesney, who met them with caustic remarks that caused them to grin despite their weariness and pain. Slade and Parker betook themselves to the Hogwaller for something to eat, where they were greeted uproariously.

Wingless Angel sat with them at table and had to be regaled with an account of what happened, Parker being nothing loath to oblige. Wingless spread the story at the bar and men came over to shake hands with Slade and compliment him on his exploit.

"Old Jim McNelty himself couldn't have handled it better," one veteran declared. "That's where you belong, son, with the Rangers, instead of mavericking around."

Val Parker, who could see deeper into the trunk of a tree than most, chuckled, and winked at Slade.

"Going to tell anybody else about Curtis?" he asked, when they had a moment alone. Slade shook his head.

"No, I don't think so, for two reasons," he replied. "First, there is always the faint possibility that I might be wrong, in which case I'd be doing the man a grave injustice. Secondly, if I take too many people into my confidence, no matter how trustworthy they may be, somebody is liable to let something slip. I don't think Curtis suspects that I've read his brand aright, which is to my advantage. Let him get suspicious and he is very likely to cover up, or even pull out. And so far I haven't any reliable evidence against him. He may be already contemplating doing just that; but if so, I think he'll try to make one good haul before he does. That's what I'm counting on, heavily; it's part of my hunch, the real foundation of it in fact. So I'm going to play it to the hilt."

"I'd sure like to be along when the showdown comes," Parker said. "I've got a score to settle with that hellion on account of what he tried to do to Ragnal."

"Perhaps you will be," Slade answered, "for I don't know for sure just yet how things are going to work out."

Tom Bowles dropped in with news.

"A bar owner from Odessa is in town, visiting a relative," said Bowles. "He had a look at those carcasses and said he distinctly remembered three of them coming into his place several times. Said they were always together and always looked as if they'd been doing some hard riding. Salty-looking customers, he said, but they were quiet and well behaved and kept to themselves."

"Stopped over in Odessa in the course of one of their trips to and from New Mexico," Slade commented. "I doubt if any of the bunch hung out in Signal much; too close to their base of operations."

"Quite likely," Bowles agreed.

When Bowles moved away a moment to talk to an acquaintance, Slade remarked to Parker, "Curtis would be too smart to allow his hellions to celebrate here. Whiskey opens a man's lips and one of them might let something slip. Odessa has never been bothered by the Henry bunch, so folks over there don't pay them any mind."

"Guess that's so," agreed Parker. "Well, at the rate things are going, folks here won't be paying the Henry bunch any mind before long either."

Before going to bed, Slade cleaned and oiled his guns. "Well, looks like we may be heading for showdown," he told the big sixes, in the habit of men who are much alone. "Yes, showdown, if things work out as I'm expecting. I only hope I don't make another fool blunder and end up

191

holding the hot end of the branding iron. Oh, well, reckon nobody is infallible; but it'll be a mighty bad time to make a mistake. Liable to be my last."

He chuckled, sheathed the irons and went to sleep with an easy mind, arising when it was still dark. After making sure he was not being watched, he got the rig on Shadow and headed west.

As he rode under the fading stars, Slade reviewed the situation as it stood. Tarp Henry, or Curtis, had lost at least ten of his bunch, and from all the information Slade had been able to gather, the outfit had not numbered many more than a dozen. So for most operating purposes, he was pretty well crippled. Wide-looping was out as an activity for the time being. And the morale of his few remaining followers must be somewhat shattered. He'd have to do something fast, something lucrative, in a hurry. Such being the case, the Ranger felt that he might well make a try for the mine he evidently believed Uncle Ben Grady knew the whereabouts of, or at least what gold the prospector might have accumulated.

Such was the hunch Slade was playing, and he believed it was a straight one. Actually it was the result of careful thought, of putting himself in Curtis's place and reasoning as he believed the outlaw leader would reason. Well, with good luck he'd find out before long. If he could reach the prospector's cabin without being detected there was a good chance that Curtis would not suspect his presence if he really was planning a raid. A raid that, he believed, would take place in short order. Well, time would tell. He rode on in a carefree mood, which was usually El Halcón's mental outlook when activity promised.

When he reached the clearing, several hours after daybreak, Slade found Uncle Ben making ready to scale the mountain for the last time. He greeted the Ranger warmly and at once set about preparing him some breakfast. Slade cared for Shadow and joined him in the cabin.

"Yep, today does it," said Uncle Ben. "I've just about cleaned her. Even though the mine was worked out, those gravel heaps sure paid off big. I've panned and stashed away a little better than two hundred pounds of metal, best I can figure it."

"Hope you've got it safely hidden," Slade remarked.

Uncle Ben chortled. "I have," he said, "in a place nobody would ever think of looking. Each night I toted my day's panning into the cabin, in plain daylight. Then well after dark, I'd slip out and bury it in the sand bank."

"That was smart," Slade agreed.

"And I'm sure glad you showed up today," said Uncle Ben. "Now you'll be along when I pack the gold to town tomorrow or the next day, whichever you say."

"We'll talk it over tonight," Slade evaded a direct reply, not wishing to definitely commit himself at the moment.

Slade ate his breakfast, Uncle Ben having coffee with him, and in a cheerful frame of mind they set out on the final trip to the mountain top. They would not have felt so complacent had they noted the hidden eyes that, peering from the growth which flanked the clearing, watched the raft bob around the bulge and out of sight. As they toiled up the worn steps, Grady eyed the broken roof of the cave with an apprehension that had never left him.

"Plumb glad this is the last trip," he said. "I'm always scairt those darn rocks will come tumbling down on my head and squash me flat."

"I think they're safe enough so long as nothing disturbs them," Slade reassured him. "Must have been that way a long time."

Reaching the mine shaft, they descended and went to work on the last heap of gravel. Mid-afternoon came and went and the final shovelful was washed. Slade hefted the bucket.

"A good day's pay, anyhow," he said. "Okay, you skin up the ladder and I'll fasten the bucket and you can haul it up. Then I'll join you and we'll head for the clearing."

Uncle Ben mounted to the outside, drew up the

bucket and sent the ladder dangling down the shaft. Slade was leaning against the rock wall, rolling a cigarette.

Suddenly from above came a stifled yell. It was Grady's voice.

Slade bounded forward and craned his neck to peer up the shaft.

"What's the matter?" he called anxiously.

The boom of a shot was the answer. A bullet fanned his face with its lethal breath. He leaped back, drawing his guns, and sent a stream of lead up the shaft. The shots were echoed by an angry yelp of pain and a torrent of curses. He went backward another step as something dark flashed down the shaft to thud solidly on the ground. A quick look and he realized what it was—the timber to which the upper end of the rope ladder had been secured. It had been shoved from the stone supports and let fall down the shaft, bringing the ladder with it. He was effectually trapped in the mine.

"All right, that takes care of him," shouted a harsh voice. "He can't get out. Leave him down there till we get the boss up here tonight and he decides what to do about him. Come on. We got the one we want."

The voices receded from the shaft. Soon Slade could no longer hear their mumble. He reloaded his guns, leaned against the tunnel wall and gave himself over to very serious thought.

"Slipped again!" he growled wrathfully. "The hellions were keeping tabs on us and figured what was going on. Well, this can very likely be my last slip."

Yes, that was it. The outlaws had hauled the raft back to the clearing, reached the hilltop and jumped Uncle Ben.

"And we'll both be goners when that sidewinder Curtis gets here," he told himself grimly. "They'll do for Ben and leave me to starve."

He gazed longingly at the shaft opening. Only twenty feet to the outside, but it might as well be twenty miles. He made plan after plan and discarded them in turn. The sides of the shaft were perfectly smooth; a lizard would have to double-head to get up them. The stone columns which had supported the long beams were too far back for him to cast a loop over, even could he hope to do so without being detected. It began to look very much like it was curtains. He rolled another cigarette and smoked it slowly, his mind still working on the problem, which apparently defied solution.

As he ground the butt out he was conscious of thirst. Well, at least he wouldn't lack for water. He groped his way to the little stream, and drank copiously.

He was still furiously angry with himself and frightfully concerned about Uncle Ben in the clutches of the sadistic devils; for he felt himself responsible for the old man's terrible predicament. What he had considered a carefully thought out and well-planned scheme had backfired with a vengeance. At his feet, the little stream seemed to chortle derisively.

21

Suddenly a thought struck him that caused his pulses to bound. The stream! He was confident it was the same body of water that gushed from the cliff face above the clearing. If it reached the outer air, maybe he could do so by way of it. The natural bore it followed was wide enough to permit his passage, and he did not believe it narrowed appreciably at any point, otherwise the flow of water from the cliff would evince greater pressure because of constriction. He recalled definitely that it tumbled straight down the face of the cliff and did not gush forward. If he got out, he'd still be some six hundred feet above the ground; getting down wouldn't be easy, perhaps impossible. That problem, however, could be left until he came face to face with it. Right now his prime objective was to reach the outer air.

Fumbling about in the dark, he finally located the lantern that had provided light by which the last gravel heap was washed. He struck a match and touched the flame to the wick. For a moment his eyes were dazzled by the transition from black dark, but they quickly adjusted themselves to the change. With renewed hope replacing what had been close to despair, he hurried down the tunnel, keeping close to the purling water and lighting his way with the lantern. There appeared to be no pitfalls and the bore maintained a uniform height and width. It looked like the first part of the hazardous journey would not be too difficult.

For a while he made good progress, although the windings of the tunnel were such that he could not be at all sure how much distance he had covered. Then without warning the lantern flame began to jump and quiver. Anxiously he shook the bowl, cursing his lack of foresight in not securing the other lantern as well; the bowl was almost empty. He increased his pace until he was almost running.

Lower and lower sank the flame. Lower still; it gave an almost human gasp and winked out. The dark rushed down upon him like a living thing.

For a moment he experienced something close to near panic, feeling an almost overpowering urge to race ahead at frantic speed. With an effort of the will he got a grip on himself, slowed his pace and strode grimly on. After all he had a guide, the gurgle and whisper of the stream. He couldn't very well get lost so long as he kept close to the water's edge.

But it was nerve-wracking work, hesitating ahead through the stygian blackness with no guarantee of what the next step forward would bring forth. His flesh crawled as he kicked a loose stone and heard it thud down a steep slope to his right and after a moment of silence send up a faint click as it hit the bottom of a chasm a tremendous distance below. He hugged the water's edge and proceeded with greater caution.

Progress in utter darkness is deceptive. It seemed to Slade that he must have covered twice the distance to the outer cliff face, even though calm reasoning told him he had not. Perhaps his judgment was wrong, that this was not the same stream which tumbled into the creek that edged the clearing below. Perhaps it wandered on and on through the bowels of the mountain until it either plunged over some tremendous precipice or dried up. In either case his fate would be a terrible one indeed.

And then, when despair was again gripping his heart, he sighted light ahead, a mere graying of the darkness but indubitably light. He quickened his step.

As he hurried forward the light quickly strengthened. A few more minutes and he was standing in a jagged opening and gazing down at the cabin in the clearing, six hundred feet and more below.

"Now if I just don't slip and bust my fool neck," he muttered as he began the hazardous descent.

However, he was strong and active, moreover experienced in rock work, and he made no slips.

And the descent of the slope was really not too difficult, although there were places that made his hair bristle on his head. But it was different when he reached the cliff wall. To his immense relief, though, he found that the cliff, which appeared absolutely sheer from below, really slanted back a little. And the plunging stream, when swollen by the rains, had in the course of ages carved little ledges and protuberances in the face of the stone. Clinging with fingers and toes, he made his slow way down the dizzy escarpment. The sun had set and the sky was flaming with color. Below, the shadows were already beginning to gather.

Finally he reached the point where the stream plunged downward over the lip of the ledge. Beyond, the cliff was absolutely sheer, and smooth as glass. And the drop was a good fifty feet to the hurrying black waters of the creek that foamed into the canyon with the speed of a mill race.

Clinging to a little jut of stone, he twisted about and gazed down. The creek was narrow, but the water was deep; he could make the drop, all right, of that he was confident. But that seething, speeding current was something else. Were it to sweep him around the bulge and into the canyon he was lost. Downstream he could glimpse the slanting shadow of the raft rope as it dipped and bobbed just below the surface. If he could catch it as he went by, he had a chance.

"Well, here goes," he muttered. Drawing a deep breath he leaped into space.

A moment of wind screeching past his ears and tearing at his clothes and he hit the surface feet first with a mighty splash. Down he went, down and down, weighted by his boots and his guns. His feet touched bottom and he began to rise, slowly, slowly. His lungs were bursting and red flashes were storming before his eyes when he broke surface, gulped in a great breath of life-giving air and shook the water from his eyes.

Then the current gripped him and he was hurled downstream at a dizzy pace. He sighted the slanting rope rushing toward him at appalling speed. Another instant and he hit it with a force that knocked the breath from his body. His clutching fingers gripped it, were torn loose. For an instant he thought he was lost. A despairing lunge and his hand gripped it again, and held.

Then began the mighty struggle up the wet strand, hand over hand, with the current buffeting him, tearing at him with liquid fingers, seeking to pluck his hold from the saving rope. For what seemed hours he fought the tossing water, blinded, gasping, half-drowned. Then he was lying on the bank, panting for breath, waves of blackness sweeping over him, flashes of light dazzling his eyes. He was on the brink of sheer exhaustion, and mighty close to being over the brink.

After a while, however, his strength came surging back. He sat up, emptied his boots of water, wrung out his clothes as best he could. From his waterproof pouch he took tobacco, papers and matches and rolled a cigarette with fingers that still trembled a bit. Taking a deep drag on the brain tablet, he looked about and considered the situation.

The clearing was devoid of sound and motion save for four horses, cinches loosened, bits flipped back, that cropped the grass. With a glance at them, Slade arose and made his way to the lean-to, where Shadow and the mules were tethered. After making sure the big black was okay, he stepped out and again glanced around, hesitating as to what was his next move. From a cunningly concealed secret pocket in his broad leather belt he slipped the famous silver star set on a silver circle, the feared and honored badge of the Texas Rangers, and pinned it to his shirt front; the time for concealment was past.

The important question was, had the boss and the outlaw who had been sent for him already arrived? The fact that but four horses were in the clearing inclined Slade to believe that they had not. If they hadn't and did while he was attempting to rescue Uncle Ben, the advantage would be on their sides, and the odds against him were already darned heavy. And had they already appeared and arrived at the hilltop, even now they might be at work on the old prospector, forcing him to talk and reveal the hiding place of his gold. He concentrated on the problem with an intensity that amounted to mental agony. And then abruptly Shadow began blowing softly through his nose, his warning to his master that other horses were approaching.

Slade slipped into a nearby clump of brush and waited, hands on the butts of his guns, peering past the cabin toward the trail.

From the growth which flanked the clearing, where the shadows were already deep, appeared two mounted men. One was a bearded giant with hard, watchful eyes. The other was Allen Curtis.

The bearded man was speaking in a loud voice, the words reaching Slade's ears.

"See?" he said. "Just like I told you. See the rope fastened to the tree? There's a raft tied to the other end of that rope. That's how the horned toads got to the top of the infernal hill. They've got the gold hid up there somewhere. We tore the cabin to pieces after we watched them pull out this morning, and couldn't find an ounce. So we followed them and grabbed Grady. And bottled up El Halcón in the mine."

"Let him stay there till he starves," Curtis said, with vicious emphasis. "Everything's gone wrong since that owl-hoot hellion showed up here. Let him starve!"

"He will," the bearded man said, with an evil

chuckle. "After we got Grady, me and Anse and Ward pulled the raft back and I came for you. They went back up the hill to help Quince and Foster keep a watch on Grady."

"You did all right," said Curtis as they dismounted and moved toward the raft. "Grady will tell us where the gold is before I get through with him. Okay, we'll haul the raft back and get going."

The bearded man gripped the rope with his huge, hairy hands. Walt Slade stepped from behind the brush, a gun in each hand. His voice rang out: "Elevate! In the name of the State of Texas, you are under arrest!"

Curtis and the other whirled at the sound of his voice, to stare unbelievingly.

"Hell and blazes!" squalled the bearded man. "He's a Ranger!"

Looking dazed, he started to raise his hands. Allen Curtis, his face a mask of hate, flashed his right hand to his left armpit.

Slade shot him, squarely between his glaring eyes. The bearded man jerked his gun and answered El Halcón shot for shot.

Back and forth through the gathering gloom gushed the red flashes. The air quivered to the reports. Then, one sodden sleeve rent and torn, blood dripping from a grazed arm and a creased cheek, Slade lowered his smoking guns and peered at the two motionless forms lying on the sand bank. In grim silence he reloaded his guns, strode forward and gripped the rope with both hands.

Getting the raft back upstream was a hefty chore for one man, but Slade's great strength, augmented by his fear for Uncle Ben, made nothing of the task. He wound the rope about the windlass and sent the clumsy craft downstream at a dizzy pace. He knew from experience that the current would hurl the raft to safety and went up the ledge at a run, fearful for old Ben and beset by a disquieting feeling that the shooting might have been heard by the outlaws on the hilltop, although he hardly thought it could have been. He mounted the steps, breathing hard, and swiftly made his way to the upper mouth of the cave, for he knew the route by heart. He paused a few moments to ease his breathing and the pounding of his heart. Then he slipped cautiously from the tunnel and peered about.

The walled cup shimmered with faint moonlight shining through a veil of cloud. Near the old cabin and close to the encroaching growth a fire glowed and flickered. He stole toward it, taking advantage of all possible cover. Behind a bush just outside the ring of light he paused.

Beside the fire sat old Ben. His hands were free but his ankles were securely bound. Grouped around him were three men who regarded him balefully.

"What's the sense of waiting for Curtis," growled a swarthy individual who nursed a bullet-gashed cheek. "I say get to work on him right now and make him tell where the stuff's hid. Maybe Pete couldn't find Curtis, or something. You going to talk, Grady?"

"I'll talk when you haul Slade outta that hole and turn him loose, not before," old Ben replied sturdily.

"We'll see about that," said the swarthy man. "Heat that hunk of iron, Anse, and give him a taste of it."

"Reckon we might as well," replied a fox-faced man with grizzled hair. "Iron's already hot."

He drew a rusty bar of iron from the fire as he spoke, the tip of which glowed red. With gloating anticipation he turned toward old Ben.

22

Into the circle of firelight strode a grim and terrible figure, face caked with dried blood, eyes like fire beneath ice, a cocked gun in each hand.

"Up!" Slade thundered. "I'm itching for an excuse to belly shoot the four of you! If I wasn't an officer of the law, I'd do it right now!"

Caught settin', numbed by the glare of the terrible eyes of El Halcón, the outlaws could do nothing but obey. They mouthed and cursed, but their hands shot up. Slade holstered one gun, fumbled a knife from his pocket, and never taking his eyes off the raging outlaws, tossed it to Grady.

"Cut yourself loose, Ben, and get their guns," he said. "Careful, now."

Uncle Ben seized the knife, flipped it open and slashed the cords that bound his ankles. He scrambled to his feet.

But he had failed to take account of his legs numbed by the tightly drawn rawhide thongs. He lurched off balance and for an instant was squarely between Slade and the four captives.

One of the outlaws took a chance; his hands swept down. He fell back with a gasping cry as Slade blazed a shot past Grady and caught him squarely in the chest. His companions, granted a second's respite, dived headlong into the brush.

Grady was reeling about like a drunken man. Slade bounded forward, gripped him by the arm and ran him out of the circle of firelight. At the same time he sent a stream of lead hissing into the brush. Yells and curses and a roar of gunfire echoed the reports. Bullets whipped past, but the outlaws shot wildly and none found a mark. Slade dragged the well-nigh helpless Grady on by main strength. More yells sounded, and more shots.

"To the cave!" Slade snapped. "It's our only chance."

They reached the cave mouth with bullets storming about their ears and dived into the black opening.

"I can make it now," gasped Uncle Ben. "Blood's back in my legs."

Together they raced along the bore. Behind them guns boomed, the reports roaring and bellowing between the rock walls. Bullets smacked against the stone and showered them with fragments as they whisked around a turn. They sped through the lofty temple-cave, where the unseen figure of Quetzalcoatl brooded in the dark, reached the stairs and bounded down them. As they reached the outer ledge, Slade abruptly halted, pulling Uncle Ben to a stop beside him. The moon was now directly overhead, the clouds had thinned away and the creek was a silvery stream of radiance.

"We've got to hold them in the cave till that moonlight clears away," Slade said. "Out there now we'd be setting quail."

He began shooting into the cave mouth as he spoke. The outlaws' guns answered, but he and Uncle Ben hugged the wall of the cliff and were untouched. The owlhoots were cursing and raving, but dared not venture out onto the moonlit ledge.

But just the same, Slade knew their position was serious. They must wait until the moon was behind the canyon wall, but as the darkness closed down, the outlaws might well take a chance and rush them; and the odds were heavy. He fired at what sounded like a cautious foot on the bottom step of the stairs. A curse echoed the report and the owl-hoot guns let go a roaring volley.

Then suddenly the booming of the guns was drowned by a horrible growling screech and an earth-shaking crash.

"Run!" Slade yelled. "The roofs falling in! The shooting's loosened the rocks!"

With death thundering at their very heels they fled down the ledge, rock fragments spewing from the cave mouth and showering all around them. Grady lost his footing and knocked Slade down as he fell. Together they rolled for bruising yards. As they scrambled frantically to their feet they realized that the uproar had abruptly ceased.

The only sound that broke the silence was a faint squealing that drifted from the cave mouth, like to the agonized cry of a stepped-on rat. Almost instantly it stilled.

"All over," Slade remarked. "They've stopped falling."

"And all over with the Tarp Henry bunch, too," quavered Uncle Ben, mopping cold drops from his forehead. "Did you hear that last squeak? It was awful! I feel sick! Let's get out of here!"

They stumbled on, and a little later breathed the sweet night air at the foot of the ledge. In silence they launched the raft and drew it upstream to the sand bank, for neither felt much like talking after the horror that had just occurred. Clean death by bullet or knife was one thing, but mangled and broken and crushed in the black dark was quite another, and not nice to speak or think about.

"Hello!" Uncle Ben exclaimed as they beached the raft. "I see you got a couple down here!"

"That's right," Slade replied. "Tarp Henry and another. Take a look at Henry—that's him lying on his back."

Uncle Ben stooped and peered at the dead face. "For the love of Pete!" he gasped. "Allen Curtis!"

"Allen Curtis, or Tarp Henry, as you prefer," Slade said. "Curtis was the head of the bunch."

Uncle Ben had straightened up and was staring at the silver star pinned to Slade's shirt front.

"So that's what you are!" he exclaimed. "Well, I should have guessed it."

"Yes, I'm a Ranger," Slade admitted. "Undercover man for McNelty's company, and as there is no real reason why I shouldn't, I'd prefer to stay undercover in this section. So if you'll forget what you just saw"—he unpinned the badge and slipped it back into its hiding place—"I'd appreciate it."

"I understand," nodded Uncle Ben. "Done forgot all about it already. Now for some hot coffee and a surrounding—that should help."

They found the cabin pretty well torn up by the outlaws searching for the gold, with even some of the floor boards removed, but the stove was intact and so were the provisions on the shelves. Uncle Ben got busy while Slade looked after the horses in the clearing and soon they sat down to an appetizing meal and plenty of steaming coffee, which did help a lot.

"Well, nobody will ever go up to the old mine again," Slade remarked as, with a contented sigh, he began manufacturing a cigarette. "But you're sitting pretty."

"Uh-huh, and do you know what I'm going to do, and pronto?" replied Uncle Ben. "I'm going to buy me a cow factory and set out all day in the sun. I never want to see another hole in the ground!"

"My sentiments precisely," Slade agreed.

"And now let's clean up and go to bed," he added. "Tomorrow we'll dig up your gold and head to town. Right now I feel like I'd been drawn through a knothole and hung on a barbed-wire fence to dry. Glad I've got a clean shirt and overalls in my pouches. I need 'em. My wounds? You mean those two scratches? The wash-up took care of them. All I want now is rest."

They straightened out the bunks and slept soundly until dawn, arising their normal selves again. After breakfast they got busy. They dug up the gold and loaded it on the mules, together with such odds and ends Uncle Ben desired to take with him. Then the bodies of Curtis and the bearded outlaw were roped to their saddles.

Slade gestured to the bearded man. "The one who posed as Tarp Henry, while Curtis directed operations, mostly in the background; he was the big fellow with the flashing black eyes folks who claimed to have seen Henry talked about."

"And they went to hell together," grunted Uncle Ben.

The other horses were left in the clearing, where they could fend for themselves until picked up. After a last look at the grim cliffs that were the tomb of the remainder of the notorious Tarp Henry bunch, they headed for town.

It was slow going with the laden mules and horses and the blaze of the sunset was over the western crags when they finally reached the cowtown. And then there was something of a to-do in Signal. Sheriff Chester, after exhausting his vocabulary of amazed profanity over Allen Curtis's body, routed out the bank cashier and the huge weight of precious metal was safely stowed in the vault. Val Parker and Ronald Ragnal were sent for and arrived long after dark on foaming horses. The Hogwaller was packed to the doors and the story of the wiping out of the Henry gang had to be told over and over, Uncle Ben doing most of the talking.

Slade was greatly pleased at the change in Ragnal. His eyes were bright, his step brisk, his bearing assured.

"Sure I'm going home," he told the Ranger. "I want to see my old Dad and show him I'm a man at last. The title? To heck with it! I'm not interested. I expect to have a nice visit and then I'm coming back to Texas. I'm going to become a Texas citizen and show Val Parker how to raise real cows."

"Oh, yes?" mocked Parker. "Compared to my stock, the scrawny little runts you'll raise will only be good for fertilizer."

With Bowles, Doc McChesney and Uncle Ben, they foregathered at the bar for a mite of celebration.

"Where's Slade?" Ragnal suddenly asked. "He was here a minute ago."

Tom Bowles, who could have provided the answer, merely smiled.

"Oh, he's around somewhere, he'll be back," said Parker.

But in the shadow of the western hills, a tall, black-haired man rode a tall black horse under the glittering stars.

"No sense in us sticking around any longer," he told the horse. "Chore's finished, and Captain Jim will have something else lined up for us by the time we get back to the post."

He rode on, singing softly in his deep, rich voice. El Halcón on the out-trail again, and happy.

Books are produced in the United States using U.S.-based materials

Books are printed using a revolutionary new process called THINKtech™ that lowers energy usage by 70% and increases overall quality

Books are durable and flexible because of Smyth-sewing

Paper is sourced using environmentally responsible foresting methods and the paper is acid-free

Center Point Large Print
600 Brooks Road / PO Box 1
Thorndike, ME 04986-0001 USA

(207) 568-3717

US & Canada:
1 800 929-9108
www.centerpointlargeprint.com